Love, Lessons, Lies,

and the Game of Life

Book 2:

The Becoming

by Dr. Charmaine Marie, Ed.D.

Published by: Real LOVE Publications

Love, Lessons, and the Game of Life Book 2:

The Becoming

by Dr. Charmaine Marie, Ed.D.

ISBN#: 979-8-9945311-0-5

Printed in the United States of America

Thank you for taking the time to read,

Love, Lessons, and the Game of Life Book 2:

The Becoming

We hope you enjoy the book.

Please do a book review on Amazon.com

to let us know what you think.

Book 1 Recap

Love, Lessons, Lies, and the Book of Life: Book 1

I'm Marie Tucker. The woman with two men. Marcellus has been my heart since I was sixteen; my first love, my safe place, my always. What started as something innocent grew into a love that felt written long before I ever understood destiny. Marcellus is my king in the truest sense.

Then there's Dupree. What was meant to be a moment, fire, rebellion, a one-night distraction, turned into something deeper than I ever planned. He came into my life with edge and intensity and somehow stayed with love just as real. Different, yes. But real.

People like to call this chaos. I call it truth.

Book One is the story of how we got here, how love, loyalty, desire, mistakes, and timing all collided. It's the building of an empire, the choosing of each other over the noise of the world, and the lessons learned through heartbreak, passion, and survival. It's raw. It's messy. It's honest.

This is where the foundation was laid; through love, lies, and lessons I didn't ask for but needed.

Prologue to Book 2

This is where becoming begins.

I'm still Marie Tucker. Still loving Marcellus. Still connected to Dupree. But I'm no longer the same woman you met before. Book Two isn't about how I loved, it's about how I learned.

The back-and-forth doesn't disappear, but the blind spots do. The truths get heavier. The choices get clearer. The standards get higher. I start seeing men, love, and myself without the rose-colored glasses. What once felt exciting now demands accountability. What once felt familiar now has to earn its place.

This is the season where I level up emotionally, spiritually, and mentally. I stop surviving love and start mastering it. This book walks through the time where I come into my own; wiser, stronger, and far less willing to settle. The love is still there, but so are the consequences. And not everyone grows at the same pace.

This isn't about losing love. It's about learning how to hold it without losing myself. Welcome to the next chapter of my life: same heart, sharper vision, and higher stakes.

Chapter One

The airport was crowded with the usual chaos, but Marie's mind was a whirlwind of its own. She felt a heaviness in her chest of yet another heartbreak as she rode down the escalator, her mind replaying the reality of Marcellus' betrayal. Marie took a deep breath as the ground floor approached, bracing for the loneliness that awaited her.

Then, out of the blue, Marie heard a smooth, confident voice. She turned to see a man standing a few steps away. His presence was striking. He wore a green Adidas tracksuit with white stripes, matching white Adidas shoes with green stripes, and a crisp white Kangol hat with a green logo. His smile was warm, and his demeanor was calm yet commanding.

"Hey there, Beautiful," he greeted, his voice smooth as velvet. "I saw you on that plane. Your style caught my eye, but you looked stressed. Everything alright? Mind if I call you Beautiful?"

Marie felt her lips curve into a small smile despite herself. "No, Sir, I don't mind," she replied softly. "Stressed doesn't even cover it, but I'm hanging in there."

The man chuckled, a sound that felt like a warm embrace. "Not 'Sir,'" he corrected playfully. "Just Terrence. Do I look that old to you?"

Marie laughed, "No, you don't look old at all. Nice to meet you, Terrence."

"Likewise, Beautiful," Terrence said, his eyes never leaving Marie. "Now, let me be straight with you, you need a man. I'm that man."

The boldness of Terrence's words caught Marie off guard, but there was something about him that made her feel safe, seen, and oddly comforted. His confidence was magnetic, and though she saw through his smooth talk, she was too weary to push him away.

"Are you from Omaha?" Marie asked, curious about this charismatic stranger.

"No, my oldest daughter just got stationed in Bellevue," Terrence explained. "She graduated from Air Force boot camp, so I'm here to check on her."

"That's amazing. How old is she?" Marie inquired.

"She's 19," Terrence answered, pride evident in his voice. "I have three daughters 14, 4, and my eldest."

"Wow," Marie said, genuinely impressed.

"Do you have any kids?" Terrence asked.

"No, I'm just twenty-seven," Marie replied, her voice tinged with the vulnerability she rarely shared.

Terrence nodded thoughtfully. "I had my first daughter at 15. Not planned, but my choice based on my decisions."

Marie absorbed Terrence's words, appreciating his honesty. There was a depth to Terrence, a story behind the swagger that intrigued her.

"I'm going to give you my number," Terrence said, slipping a card into Marie's hand. "This is for you, not your man, so keep it safe."

Marie chuckled, shaking her head. "No one cares if I have a number."

"Somebody cares," Terrence replied, his tone softening. "I'll be here for three days. If you have time, get at me."

As Terrence walked away, Marie clutched the card tightly. For the first time today, she felt desirable, seen, and appreciated. Terrence's words had a way of seeping into her heart, mending the cracks Marcellus had left behind.

Although Marie knew she couldn't bring someone like Terrence home to her family, the thought of spending time with him brought a smile to her face.

He was captivating, a smooth talker with the kind of swag that made her forget her pain, even if just for a moment.

As Marie stepped into her jitney, she realized something profound, she didn't need a man to tell her she was beautiful. But it sure felt good when someone like Terrence did.

Chapter Two

After stepping out of the jitney, Marie entered her home and immediately felt the quiet embrace of solitude. The chaos of her thoughts began to settle as she moved through the familiar space. She lit a few scented candles, their gentle glow casting a warm, calming light across the room. Soft jazz music filled the air, each note soothing Marie's frayed nerves, creating a sanctuary where she could finally breathe.

Marie ran a hot bubble bath, the steam rising like a balm for her soul. This was her ritual, her sacred time to reconnect with herself. Slipping into the warm water, she felt the tension begin to melt away. The worries, the hurt, and the betrayal she had carried seemed to dissolve with each passing minute.

Marie allowed herself to simply be; no distractions, no demands, just her and the comforting embrace of the water. For 45 minutes, she stayed in that bath, letting her mind wander, her thoughts flowing freely like the gentle ripples around her. It was in this moment that Marie reclaimed a piece of herself, finding solace in the quiet.

When she finally emerged, her skin warmed and softened, she wrapped herself in a plush towel, feeling lighter, as if the water had washed away more than just the day's grime. Marie slipped into something comfortable and made her way to the bed, with the soft fabric of the bedspread inviting her to rest.

Lying on top of the bed, Marie surrendered to the pull of sleep, allowing her body to fully relax for the first time in what felt like forever. For three hours, she drifted into a deep, peaceful slumber. It wasn't just rest, it was true peace, a declaration that Marie deserved this moment of self-love and tranquility.

When Marie woke up, she felt rejuvenated, her spirit steadied. She had given herself permission to let go, to pause, and to heal. In that act of self-care, she found the strength to rise again, ready to face whatever life had in store. This was more than just a nap, it was a reclaiming of her power, a reminder that she could find peace within herself whenever she needed it.

Chapter Three

In the dim light of her living room, Marie lounged on the couch, the hum of the television was a soft background to her thoughts. Her phone rang, pulling her from her relaxing moment.

"Hello?" she answered, her voice weary but curious.

"What's up, Cuz?" Charlotte's familiar voice rang through.

"Hey, Charlotte. Not much, just lying here, trying to relax and watch some TV," Marie replied, as a tired smile crept onto her face. "What about you? It's been a minute."

"Yeah, a lot's been going on. But you sound like you've got something on your mind," Charlotte said, cutting straight to the point.

Marie exhaled and a small laugh escaped. "You could say that. Just trying to unwind, you know? But it's not exactly working."

"Spill it, girl. You know you can't just tease me like that. Come on, let's grab some food and talk. Perkins at 7:00 PM?" Charlotte suggested, her tone warm yet insistent.

Marie felt her stomach growl at the mention of food. "Seven sounds perfect. I'm starving," she admitted, her voice gaining a bit of enthusiasm.

Hanging up, Marie quickly freshened up, slipping into a pair of jeans, a fitted t-shirt, and her favorite rhinestone sandals. A touch of lip gloss and some earrings later, Marie was ready, car keys in hand and all.

Chapter Four

Marie's phone rang right as she was about to walk out the door.

Ring Ring Ring!

She answered on the third ring. "Hello?"

"Hey, what's up, Marie?"

"Not much, Brie. What you doing?"

"Nothing really. I'm on my way to go grab something to eat with Charlotte. I was just about to walk out the door."

"Oh okay, well I hope y'all have fun."

"Yeah, we will. Thank you."

I was just calling to check on you to see how you've been doing."

"I'm good," Marie said, chuckling. "Life is doing what life does."

"Same," Brielle replied. "I tried calling Catherine and Tasha, too. I was trying to see if we could all get on the phone together, but nobody answered."

Marie chuckled. "That sounds about right."

"I know, right?" Brielle said. "Everybody's busy. We keep saying we're gonna get together and never do."

"We really do need to, though," Marie said. "But you know how life gets."

"Exactly," Brielle agreed. "That's why I just wanted to check in and make sure you're good."

"I appreciate that," Marie said sincerely. "Things are good on my end. I don't have any complaints."

"That's good to hear," Brielle said. "I just wanted to say I love you and hope you have a great week."

Marie smiled, leaning against the counter. "I love you too, friend. And same to you."

"Alright then. I'll talk to you later."

"Okay. Bye, Brie."

"Bye."

※※※※※※※※※※※※※※※※※

"Brielle just made my day. I really do appreciate when my friends call to check on me, just because they love me. I love the way we love each other in our little circle. It's simple, it's genuine, and it means so much to me. Alright, let me walk out this door so I can go eat with Charlotte."

Chapter Five

At the restaurant, Charlotte and Marie were quickly seated in a cozy booth. Menus in hand, the waitress soon arrived with their drinks, leaving them to their conversation.

"So, what's got you all twisted up?" Charlotte asked, leaning in with a knowing look.

Marie sighed, the words tumbling out. "Charlotte, you won't believe it. Marcellus called me the night before the Super Bowl. He sent me a ticket because he wanted me there for the game. It all seemed so perfect. The room was set, the game was intense, and after, we had this amazing night together. I was on cloud nine, thinking I was his one and only."

Charlotte raised an eyebrow, sensing the storm brewing beneath Marie's calm exterior.

"But then," Marie continued, her voice hardening, "the next morning, we're at the airport, and I am all smiles, and there she is, Vanessa, on Marcellus' arm, like nothing's wrong. She spotted me, and it was on. She came up, throwing accusations, asking if I was with him, and if he was with me. It was a scene."

Charlotte's eyes widened. "Girl, what did you do?"

"I was stunned. Marcellus tried to calm her down, but the damage was done. I'm standing there, blindsided. He didn't even warn me she'd be around. And then she's in my face, all attitude, acting like she owns him," Marie vented, her frustration was apparent.

Charlotte nodded slowly. "That's a lot. But Marie, didn't you say you and Marcellus have an understanding? He's your man, and you're good when you're together, and as long as he treats you right, that's all that matters, right?"

Marie hesitated. "Yeah, but it still felt wrong. He made it seem like he was just there for the money. Now, I'm not so sure. And the way she came at me, I just can't shake it."

"Look," Charlotte interjected, her tone firm but gentle, "Marcellus flew you out on the biggest night of his life. He chose you to be there. Vanessa might be around, but she wasn't with him that night. You were. Doesn't that tell you something?"

Marie bit her lip, the truth sinking in. "I guess you're right. I didn't think about it like that. I've been so caught up in my own head."

Charlotte smirked. "And speaking of your head, what about Dupree? You've got your own thing going on. Don't act like you're innocent here."

Marie rolled her eyes. "Dupree's different. And yeah, I saw him before I left. But that's not the point."

"Isn't it?" Charlotte teased. "Marie, you're living your life, making your choices. Don't get caught up in the drama. Enjoy the ride.

Speaking of rides, when I got back and was sulking at the airport on the way to my jitney, I was approached by a grown man named Terrence." Marie mentioned.

"A grown man? You're grown!" Charlotte said.

"No, Charlotte, he was a man, a real handsome man," Marie replied.

"Wow!" Charlotte said, eagerly waiting for more of the story.

"Wow is right. He's in town for a few days. He gave me his business card. He's smooth, Charlotte. Real smooth."

Charlotte leaned in, her eyes twinkling with intrigue. "Let me see that card. Looks like you've got another adventure lined up."

Marie handed the card over, her grin playful and full of mischief. "Maybe I do. But first, I need food. I need to be fully charged for whatever's coming next."

Charlotte examined the card with her eyebrows shooting up in surprise. "Wait, this guy sells houses and he's an investor?"

Marie nodded, smirking. "Yup. And he's interested in me. He's only here for three days, though."

Charlotte raised an eyebrow, her expression skeptical but intriguing. "Well, I'm not sure what exactly he's interested in, but you definitely need to meet up with him. Get to know this guy a bit more."

Marie chuckled. "Oh, trust me, I plan to."

Charlotte shot her a warning look. "Just don't be reckless. You barely know him. Meet somewhere public, not in some random hotel room."

Marie laughed, rolling her eyes. "I got it, Cuz. Don't worry."

The two burst into laughter, finishing up their meal. Charlotte picked up the tab, and they left Perkins, heading home with a fresh chapter of drama waiting to unfold.

Chapter Six

Marie drifted into a deep, peaceful sleep after her long day filled with a rejuvenating bath, a hearty lunch with her cousin Charlotte, and a much-needed nap. The soft glow of the TV flickered in the background, casting shadows across the room. All was quiet until her phone rang, breaking the silence. The clock read 1:42 AM

Ring Ring. The phone rang.

Half-asleep, Marie groggily answered, "Hello?"

"Hey, Babe," Marcellus's voice was soft and filled with regret. "I'm so sorry for waking you. I just needed to call and tell you I love you, and I apologize. I know yesterday was a lot, especially after you saw me with Vanessa at the airport. I should've told you. I should've explained everything before you found out that way. She wasn't even supposed to come; she just tagged along. It wasn't planned."

Marie, still groggy, responded, "Okay."

"Marie," Marcellus sighed, his voice heavy with emotion. "Don't 'okay' me. I know when you say it like that, you don't really mean it. Please, don't be passive."

"I'm not being passive," Marie replied softly. "I'm just trying to process everything. I heard what you said. But what I saw was different. She was in my space, Marcellus. It felt disrespectful, and I only did what you asked. It backfired."

"Marie," Marcellus said earnestly, "that night was so important to me. I needed you there, more than you know. Even if you weren't front and center, just knowing you were in the room gave me strength. You fuel me. I perform my best when you're around."

"I get that," Marie murmured, trying to keep her emotions in check. "But we need better communication. I wouldn't put you in a situation where you'd feel blindsided. It hurt."

"I know," Marcellus admitted. "Vanessa's involvement isn't what it seems. Yes, she's around, but it's temporary. You're my future. Trust me. We had a pact, remember? It's about us, not outsiders. I'm building something for us."

Marie sighed, the tension easing slightly. "I'll trust you, Marcellus. I'm holding on."

"Thank you," Marcellus said softly. "I know it's hard, but I promise, you won't regret it. I needed to call you tonight. We had a team event earlier that lasted all day, and I wasn't able to call. As soon as I could, I called you. I had to. You mean everything to me."

Marie smiled faintly. "I'm glad you did. I appreciate you calling."

They shared a moment of silence, both soaking in the reassurance of their bond.

"Marie," Marcellus said, "thank you for standing by me, and for not making a scene. You could've, but you didn't. That means everything."

"It's always been you, Marcellus," Marie said, her voice filled with quiet conviction. "Always."

"It's us," Marcellus promised. "Forever and a day."

They both laughed softly, the tension easing further. After exchanging sweet words and "I love yous," they said their goodbyes. Marcellus assured Marie he'd be home soon, and they'd have more time together.

As the call ended, Marie stayed awake, the glow of the TV casting a gentle light on her face. For the next forty-five minutes, she replayed her and Marcellus' conversation in her mind, the love, the passion, the lingering uncertainty. Finally, she drifted back into sleep, her heart a little lighter, but her mind still racing with the complexities of love and trust.

Chapter Seven

Marie dragged herself out of bed, groaning as she prepared for another hectic week. The three-day weekend had been a whirlwind, but work beckoned. Her sanctuary? A perfectly crafted cup of coffee: cinnamon, honey, ginger, cream, and a dollop of whipped cream. It was her morning ritual, a moment of peace before the chaos.

Dressed sharply in her business attire, Marie strutted to her car, the morning sun sparkling off the windshield. The Ricky Smiley Morning Show filled her commute with familiar laughter, a comforting backdrop to her thoughts.

At the office, Marie greeted her colleagues with practiced ease. Her office, a blend of royal blue and Tiffany blue, was her haven, scented with Bath & Body Works plugins. She barely had time to settle before her phone rang.

"Hello?"

"Marie, are you at work?" Catherine's voice was tight and anxious.

"Yeah, just got here. What's up?"

"We need to talk. Can I come by?"

Marie smirked, sensing Catherine's tension. "Sure, come on over. I'll let the front know."

Minutes later, Catherine entered, visibly rattled. Marie's usual nonchalant demeanor faltered. "Catherine, what's going on? You look shaken."

"I'm pregnant, Marie."

Marie blinked, her initial reaction harsh and unfiltered. "What? That's awful."

Catherine did a double-take, hurt. "Awful? How could you say that?"

Marie crossed her arms. "We agreed, no kids until we were established. This wasn't the plan."

Catherine's voice sharpened. "Maybe it wasn't your plan, but it's happening. And I thought you'd be supportive, not selfish."

Marie sighed, her tone still dismissive. "There are options, you know."

"Options?" Catherine's anger flared. "You think this is a joke? I'm serious, Marie. I love Dakar, and we've talked about a future together. This isn't just about me."

Realization dawned on Marie. She softened, guilt seeping into her voice. "I'm sorry, Catherine. I didn't mean to be so cold. I'm here for you. What do you want to do?"

"I want to tell Dakar in a special way. Maybe a quiet dinner, just the two of us."

Marie's eyes lit up with excitement. "Or, what if we made it a big surprise? A party at a restaurant, and tell everyone at once!"

Catherine shook her head. "No, Marie. Dakar deserves to know privately first. Then, we can celebrate."

Marie nodded, understanding at last. "Okay. However, you want to do it, I'm here for you. I'll support you every step of the way."

Catherine stood, her emotions still a whirlwind but softened by Marie's change of heart. They hugged tightly, a bond reaffirmed.

As Catherine left, Marie sat in her office, the weight of the moment sinking in. Despite the initial shock, excitement bubbled up. Their group had never faced something like this, but they would rally together. This baby would be loved, cherished, and celebrated.

Chapter Eight

Marie's day had been smooth, filled with productive client meetings and a serene sense of satisfaction. She was just settling into a quiet moment when her phone rang.

"Hey, Cuz! What's up?" Marie said answering her phone.

"Hey, Marie. We got two more days! Charlotte's voice was lively, almost too lively. When are we doing dinner?"

Marie sighed, already sensing where this conversation was heading. "Charlotte, stop."

"What? No, seriously. Terrence is here for two more days. You got his business card, right? The man runs businesses. He's an investor and sells houses! We need to see what he's about. That's a man."

Marie rolled her eyes, leaning back in her chair. "Charlotte, whatever happened to the cousin who gave me all that great advice? You used to tell me who to avoid and how to stay out of trouble. Now you're practically pushing me into it."

Charlotte's voice turned sharp, almost aggressive. "Marie, come on! You've got two days! Just check him out. Don't be so uptight."

Marie took a deep breath, unwilling to argue further. "Fine. We'll see. Talk later."

After hanging up, Marie sat in thought, debating whether to follow through on Charlotte's suggestion. Her mind wandered, but soon, she decided to make the call.

Chapter Nine

"Ring, ring."

"Hello, Terrence Marquice."

"Hello, Terrence. This is Marie."

There was a pause, and then Terrence's voice, smooth and inviting, filled the line. "I'm surprised, but pleasantly so. How are you, Beautiful?"

Marie felt a blush creeping in. "I'm doing great, thanks. I just thought I'd give you a call since I had your business card, and you're leaving soon."

Terrence chuckled, a deep, comforting sound. "I didn't think you'd call. Thought you might miss this train. But here we are."

Marie laughed softly. "Well, I didn't want to miss out."

They chatted effortlessly, their conversation filled with light-hearted teasing and genuine interest.

"So, what's your plan for tonight?" Terrence asked.

"I don't have any plans yet," Marie admitted.

"How about dinner?" Terrence's tone was casual but hopeful.

"Dinner sounds great. I get off at 3:00 PM today." Marie replied, excitement bubbling under her calm exterior.

"I can pick you up. I have a rental, and I promise to have you home early. No funny business."

Marie smiled, appreciating Terrence's straightforwardness. "That sounds perfect. What time?"

"How about 5:30 PM? That gives you a little time to relax after work."

"Perfect. I'll be ready."

Terrence and Marie's conversation ended with mutual anticipation. On Terrence's end, he felt a sense of satisfaction. "She's smart and charming. I can tell she's got a good upbringing. I can't wait to spend more time with her."

Marie, meanwhile, sat in a daze, her thoughts swirling around Terrence's deep voice and the way he made her feel safe, respected, and excited for something new. This wasn't the usual late-night hangout she was used to. This was different, and she liked it. Marie felt herself being drawn to this man who seemed to promise stability and sincerity, a refreshing change.

Marie sighed, smiling to herself, already imagining how the evening would unfold.

Chapter Ten

Marie pulled into the driveway of her apartment complex, her body weary from a long day at work. As she cut the engine, her eyes caught sight of a familiar car parked just a few feet away. Her heart instantly skipped a beat, and a wide grin spread across her face.

Without a second thought, Marie jumped out of her car, her excitement was bubbling over. She hurried over to Dupree's car, knocked on the window, and waited. When he looked up, his face lit up with that signature smile that always made Marie's heart flutter. He stepped out of the car, and before either of them could say a word, they embraced, their laughter filling the air.

Dupree pulled Marie close, planting a soft kiss on her lips. Their laughter and joy were real, their bodies swaying together in an unspoken rhythm of love and familiarity.

"Um, what's up, Babe? My Barak," Marie teased, her eyes sparkling with affection.

"My Michelle," Dupree replied smoothly, pulling Marie in for another hug.

Marie playfully pushed him back with a smirk on her face. "What are you doing? You can't just pull up to my house like that. You can't be doing that!" Marie said smiling. "You don't know what I got going on or who I got coming over."

Dupree chuckled, his confidence was radiating. "You don't ever have anybody in your house. I know if I can't come to your house and hang out, ain't nobody else coming over hanging out."

Marie couldn't help but laugh. "Okay, okay, okay. But still, you pulling up, you don't know what I got going on."

"You don't have anything going on. That's what I know," Dupree said, his eyes twinkling with playful certainty.

"Yeah, okay," Marie said, shaking her head. "Anyways, what's up? It's good to see you."

"It's good to see you, too," Dupree replied, his gaze locking with Marie's. "With your fine and pretty self. You didn't even call me to say you're back. What's up? You just left that morning, and that was it. I haven't heard from you at all."

Marie tilted her head, a soft smile on her lips. "I didn't hear from you either. But here we are, right? Remember, we do this. When we're together, we're together. And that's what it is. And right now, we're together. But I got something going on tonight. I have to go get dressed, and head out. I'll be back later, though. It won't be too late."

Dupree raised an eyebrow, a mischievous grin spreading across his face. "Well, what's up? What you doing when you get back?"

Marie leaned in closer, her voice dropping to a sultry whisper. "You," she said, her body moving in a slow, teasing motion. "And everything you need me to do."

Dupree's grin widened, his eyes darkening with desire. "Okay, then. That's what I'm talking about. So, when you get back, you let me know, and I'm coming to get you."

"Okay," Marie said, her smile growing. "And I'm gonna call you. I can't wait to see you."

"Yeah," Dupree replied, pulling Marie in for one last embrace. "So, we can make life happen again like we did the other day."

They both laughed, their joy infectious. After a quick kiss on the lips, Marie reluctantly pulled away, her heart was still dancing from their encounter.

As she walked toward her apartment, a big smile spread across her face. Anytime Marie saw Dupree, she couldn't help but feel a deep, inner happiness. His presence was like a soothing balm to her soul, and their love, filled with laughter and passion, made her feel alive. In that moment, everything else faded away, leaving only the warmth of their connection.

Chapter Eleven

As soon as Marie stepped through the door, the house phone started ringing. She dropped her bag and hurried over.

"Hello?"

"Hey, Marie! It's Tasha, girl. What are you doing?"

"Just walked in the house," Marie said, already heading toward her bedroom. "I'm about to get ready and head out on a date, Girl."

"Alright now!" Tasha cheered Marie on. "I saw you called earlier. I was tied up at work all day and missed you."

"I figured," Marie said. "I knew you'd call when you got a minute."

"I said let me call back and check on Marie, see how you were doing, and wish you a good week," Tasha said. "You know how we do."

"I know," Marie smiled. "And I appreciate it. I want to wish you an amazing week too. I'm about to go get cute and see how this night goes. I'll fill you in later."

"Go have fun. We'll catch up soon; you, me, Brie, and Catherine, it's overdue."

"Very overdue," Marie agreed. "We'll make it happen soon."

"Love you, Girl."

"Love you too."

They hung up, and Marie shook her head with a soft smile as she headed to get dressed, grateful for friends who checked in, even when life was moving fast. She walked to her room, singing That's What Friends Are For.

Chapter Twelve

Marie was humming with excitement as she prepared for her date with Terrence. She carefully selected a stunning red evening gown that flowed elegantly to the floor, pairing it with shiny red heels that matched perfectly. Her dangling red earrings sparkled with every movement, and a spritz of her favorite Tommy Girl perfume completed her look. She styled her hair in a sharp updo, leaving a few delicate strands out that framed her face. With her lips glossed to a luminous shine, Marie felt radiant and ready for an unforgettable evening.

At precisely 5:15 PM, Terrence pulled up in front of Marie's place. He gave her a quick call to let her know he had arrived. True to his gentlemanly nature, he stepped out of the car and walked around to the passenger side, ready to open the door for Marie.

When Marie got outside, her eyes met Terrence's, who was impeccably dressed in a silk black and royal blue Adidas jogger set, complete with matching sneakers and a royal blue Kangol hat. He smelled divine, the scent of his cologne adding to his allure.

"Wow," Terrence exclaimed, his eyes lighting up as he took in Marie's appearance. "Look at you, Beautiful. You look absolutely spectacular."

"Thank you, Terrence," Marie responded, her cheeks flushing slightly. "And you look fly as always."

They shared a warm hug before Terrence opened the car door for Marie. As they headed downtown to Cascio's Steakhouse, the atmosphere in the car was light and filled with the soft strains of blues music. Their conversation flowed effortlessly, setting the tone for a night of connection and discovery.

The restaurant was an elegant haven, with dim lighting and a serene ambiance. Once seated, they delved into a meaningful conversation. Terrence leaned in, genuinely curious, "So, Marie, tell me about yourself."

Marie smiled. "Well, I have a close relationship with my parents, three amazing best friends, and I work as a mental health counselor. It's my passion to help people reconnect with themselves and navigate through their struggles."

Terrence was impressed. "That's incredible. What are your dreams for the future?"

"Well, I've been thinking about opening my own mental health counseling practice." Marie started. "I love working at Bergen Mercy, but eventually, I'd like to have my own location in a private intimate space where clients feel safe and confident coming to me without worrying about being seen or judged."

"That's an amazing goal. When do you think you'll make that happen?" Terrence responded.

"Honestly, I hadn't thought that far ahead. It's an idea I've had for about a year, but no one's ever asked me about it until now. Talking about it makes me realize it's something I can actually achieve. I'll definitely need to explore it further."

"You should. You never know where opportunities might lead. I'm an investor, and who knows? This could be something I'd invest in."

"Wow, really?" Marie questioned surprised. "I noticed your card says you're an investor, but what does that involve?"

"I invest in properties and stocks. I buy homes, sell them, and hold onto my stocks to let them grow over time. It's been a great way to build wealth."

"How did you get into that?"

"I was in the military, but due to some medical issues, I had to leave. After that, I connected with friends who were into investing. They taught me the ropes, and I've been doing it ever since."

Marie smiled softly. "I have to be honest with you, Terrence. When I first saw you at the airport, looking all fly, I made a snap judgment. I thought, 'He's probably a dough boy, someone I could never bring home to my parents.' But there was something about you, your charm, that made me want to see you again."

Terrence raised an eyebrow, clearly surprised. "A dough boy? Really? Do I give off that vibe? I just enjoy dressing well and smelling good, and Adidas happens to be my favorite brand. Even my cologne is Adidas."

Marie shook her head quickly. "No, I apologize. You don't give off that vibe at all. I guess I was just projecting based on what I'm used to. But you exude grown man energy, and I realize now how wrong I was to judge you so quickly. You're truly something special."

Terrence smiled, his expression softening. "Apology accepted, Beautiful. No harm done. I get it."

They both laughed, the tension easing as they shared a genuine moment of understanding.

Marie and Terrence laughed and talked for hours, thoroughly enjoying each other's company. The food was incredible, and the service was exceptional.

As they finished their meal, Terrence leaned in slightly. "So, Marie, I hope this isn't the last time I see or talk to you."

Marie smiled. "Oh no, I was hoping I made a great impression. I definitely want to see you again, and again, and again."

They both laughed, sharing a moment of mutual understanding.

Terrence grinned. "How about breakfast tomorrow? What time do you have to be at work in the morning?"

Marie thought for a moment. "That sounds great! How about 7:00 AM? I don't have anything until 10:00 AM, so I can go to work after we eat."

"Seven in the morning works perfectly," Terrence replied. "I don't leave until 3:00 PM. I'm taking my daughter to lunch before I go, but you'd be the icing on my cake."

Marie chuckled. "Let's meet at Charie's Sunshine Café, at 7:00 AM."

"I'll be there," Terrence confirmed with a smile.

ƧƧƧƧƧƧƧƧƧƧƧƧƧƧ

Terrence paid the bill, and he and Marie both thanked the waiter for the excellent service. As they walked out, they handed their ticket to the valet. When their car arrived, they tipped the valet, got in, and drove off.

When they arrived at Marie's place, she started to get out of the car.

Terrence stopped her with a gentle question. "Have you opened a door since we've been together tonight?"

Marie paused and smiled. "No, I haven't."

"That's right," Terrence said, as he got out and walked around to open her door. "And you never have to when you're with me."

Terrence helped Marie out of the car and gave her a warm hug. "Thank you for an amazing night, Marie."

Marie smiled up at him. "And thank you, Terrence. I truly enjoyed everything. You are amazing."

As Marie walked to her apartment, she felt like a million dollars. She couldn't believe that after such an expensive dinner, Terrence didn't even hint at taking her back to his hotel and he didn't mention anything about sex.

She smiled to herself, thinking, That's some grown man stuff. Wow! Feeling special, Marie entered her apartment with a renewed sense of appreciation for the night.

Chapter Thirteen

Alright, y'all, I'm back to break this down a little. Let me be real with you. Terrence! Now that's a man right there. He looks good, smells amazing, dresses sharp, and has his own thing going on. From what I can tell, he's got his life together. I don't know all the details about where he lives, but he's an investor who buys and sells houses. If he's in the real estate game like that, he's got to have his own place. Right? But honestly, I don't even know where this man lives, and I know next to nothing about him.

But let me tell you, that is a man. He didn't try anything inappropriate, no touching, no sexual comments, none of that. He wasn't staring at my body or making me feel uncomfortable in any way. He didn't say a word about my breasts or my butt. There were no suggestive remarks or dirty talk. None. I felt respected, like a grown woman in his presence.

Terrence said all he wanted was a good conversation. And let me tell you, he was not lying. That's all he wanted, and it was incredible. I genuinely enjoyed myself tonight, and I'd love to experience that again. This is what I'm talking about: a man who knows how to treat a woman. I've never had that before.

Now, don't get me wrong, I still like what I like, but tonight was different. It was refreshing. And I have to admit, even though I'm raving about Terrence right now, y'all already know what's about to happen, I'm about to call Dupree. I'm hooked on him, but I just had to let y'all in on how I'm feeling because, man, Terrence is something else. He's a grown freaking man, and I'm feeling him.

Chapter Fourteen

Ring, ring.

"Hello?" Dupree answered.

"Hey, Dupree," Marie said, her voice soft yet firm. "Where you at? What you doing? I'm trying to come through."

"Okay, okay, Marie, hold on a minute," Dupree responded, his tone shifting.

In the background, Marie could hear a woman's voice yelling. Her heart sank.

"Marie? Who is that?" The woman demanded. "What you mean, hold on? Whoever that is, you need to tell them you're with somebody."

"Marie," Dupree said, sounding caught off guard. "I'm not doing nothing. Just handling some business.

"Who is that?" Marie asked.

"That's someone playing games," Dupree responded. "You know how y'all do."

The woman in the background chimed in, "I'm not playing games! You always want someone to be quiet, Dupree. But not this time."

Marie's patience snapped. "Why did you even answer the phone if you're with someone? Come on now, Dupree. What's going on?"

Dupree sighed. "Alright, Marie. I'm about to tell you where to meet me. Give me fifteen minutes, I'll call you right back."

"Okay, Dupree," Marie replied, upset and frustrated.

They hung up, and Marie sat in silence, her thoughts racing. This is what I get for dealing with Dupree. Every time, it's the same drama. I felt so respected earlier today. But now, here I am again, caught in the middle of this mess.

Marie shook her head, trying to push away the negativity. Today was different with Terrence. No drama, no games. Just respect. But her heart still pulled her toward Dupree.

Ring, ring.

"Hey, I'm sorry about that," Dupree said. "People just be trying to play games. It's nothing. You know how it is."

"Yeah, I'm sure," Marie said, her voice cooler now. "But don't even worry about it. I'm over it."

"Come on now," Dupree coaxed. "Don't trip. Like we said, when it's us, it's us. Let's make tonight ours. I'm Barack, right? Call me Barack."

Marie chuckled despite herself. "Alright, Barack. Where we meeting?"

"Meet me at the Days Inn off North 30th. I'll see you there."

"Okay, I'll be there," Marie said, hanging up.

Chapter Fifteen

Yeah, I just need to vent for a minute. The thing about Dupree is, he's always gonna play some games. He'll make you laugh, but he'll also embarrass you. He'll make you so mad you wanna wring his neck, but somehow, I still love him. I love him. He's so fine, so smooth, and so sexy. And he's a good man, a really good man, but he's got too many women hanging around, and he loves that attention.

I keep telling myself he knows how to treat me, and in some ways, he does. But there's a line, and he crosses it. It's disrespectful, and I shouldn't have to put up with it. I don't make him deal with anything like that. So why should I? I don't get it.

I'm pissed off right now. But here's the thing: I let him call me. I let him come around because I love him. I can't lie. I love the way he hugs me, kisses me, and makes me feel. And when we're together, it's magical. We'll spend the night making love, laughing, and just being in the moment, and for those few hours, it's like nothing else matters. If I could just hold on to that feeling, I wouldn't even care about the rest. But it doesn't last. The moment fades the second we're apart, and I'm left trying to figure out how to fix this.

One of these days, though, his little grin won't be enough to fix everything. He won't just get to smile his way out of the mess he creates. These women who don't know their place should know better by now. When they hear him say he's calling me, they shouldn't even dare to speak. Why do I even have to hear them? Why do they still exist in this space with me?

I'm about to check Dupree. Either he's going to set those women straight, or he's going to lose me. And I know for a fact that losing me isn't what he wants. Not even a little bit. But I'm done. Something has got to give.

Chapter Sixteen

Marie quickly got ready, showering, putting on her favorite lotion, Honeysuckle from Bath and Body Works, and dressing in her comfortable yet alluring pajamas. She drove to the Days Inn, with her mind a swirl of emotions.

When Marie arrived at the Days Inn, she called Dupree. "What room?"

"4330. Fourth floor," Dupree replied.

"Okay, I'm on my way up."

As soon as Marie stepped into the room, Dupree pulled her into a tight hug, kissing her deeply. "I'm sorry, Marie. I didn't mean to stress you out. I love you, and I'm working on being better. Let's make tonight amazing."

"No, Dupree. No." Marie shook her head, her voice firm. "I'm not about to make anything amazing. Not this time. I'm tired. I'm disappointed. I'm upset. And I'm sick of this same old pattern. Every time I call you, you're always with somebody. And you know what? It's not even the fact that you're with someone. It's the fact that they always make sure I know they're there. They always have something to say. Always trying to be seen and heard. And you let them. You disrespect me every time you do that."

"Baby, I don't disrespect you," Dupree said, his voice softer now. "I never meant to make you feel like that. I didn't even know."

"Well, now you know." Marie's tone sharpened. "Because that's exactly how I feel. It's disrespectful, it's rude, and I don't see how you let it happen. Maybe in your mind, when they start talking, you think it's just noise. But I know better. They want me to hear them. They want to be seen, like I'm supposed to get jealous, like I'm supposed to play some kind of game. But no. What it's actually doing is pushing me out the door."

Marie exhaled; her frustration was thick in the air. "I go hard for you, Dupree. I love you. I love being around you. But if I call and you're with someone else, you need to either step away to talk to me, or tell them to shut up. Because I don't want to hear them, and they shouldn't even feel comfortable speaking when they hear my name."

Dupree ran a hand over his face. "I am sorry, Marie. I really am. I didn't know it bothered you like this. You never said anything before."

"And that is exactly why I'm saying it now." Marie crossed her arms. "No more games. No more acting like this doesn't hurt me. Because it does. You think I'm fine because I smile when you come around. Because we laugh, we kick it, we have a good time. And we do. But that doesn't erase what happens when you are not with me. It doesn't erase how it makes me feel when I hear them, knowing they think they can talk slick because you allow it."

Marie looked Dupree straight in the eye. "I'm done with that. Done. If it happens again, I'm gone. I'm not moving like that no more."

Dupree nodded slowly, his expression serious now. "I understand. And I'm sorry. Really. I'm glad you're telling me because if I didn't know, I couldn't fix it. And I want to fix it. I want us to be good, Marie. I don't want to lose you."

Marie studied Dupree for a moment, searching his face. "Finally, she let out a slow breath. Alright. That's why I told you. So, we can fix it. So, we can move forward. Because I don't want to be at odds with you, Dupree. I just want to be happy with you."

Dupree stepped closer, tilting Marie's chin up before pressing a gentle kiss to her forehead. "OK,

Baby. I hear you. And I promise you, this won't happen again."

Marie nodded, feeling some of the tension ease from her shoulders. She smirked slightly. "Now what were you saying at the beginning? Something about making tonight amazing?"

Dupree grinned, his usual confidence returning. "That's what I was saying."

Marie let her fingers graze Dupree's chest before whispering, "Alright then, my Barack.

Dupree chuckled, pulling Marie closer. "Come on, my Michelle."

And just like that, the night shifted.

"I love you too," Marie whispered. "Let's make this night perfect."

Dupree smiled. "Come on, let's take a shower together."

Marie raised an eyebrow. "We've never done that before."

"First time for everything," Dupree said, taking her hand.

Marie and Dupree undressed and stepped into the shower, laughter filling the small space as they playfully teased each other. The warm water cascaded over them, washing away the tension. They shared an intimate moment filled with passion and tenderness.

Marie felt a surge of happiness and thought This is what I needed. The night unfolded beautifully, with love and connection overshadowing the earlier drama. As they lay together afterward, she knew this was one of their best nights ever.

Chapter Seventeen

Ring, ring.

"Marie! Oh my gosh! Girl, what's up? You better have something good for me. I've been waiting to hear from you! Spill it!" Charlotte blurted out, her voice full of anticipation.

Marie let out a dramatic sigh. "Oh, trust me, Char, I have a lot to tell you! But I don't have long. I'm literally on my way to breakfast with Terrence."

Charlotte gasped. "Oh my gosh! Terrence? Okay, okay. I need details now!"

Marie giggled, her excitement bubbling over. "Okay, so listen. I called him the other day, right? After you and I talked. And guess what? He asked me out to dinner. Just like that, straight to the point. No games, no hesitation. Now let me tell you what happened when I got home from work, before I got ready for my date."

Charlotte sat up. "Uh-oh. What?"

Dupree was sitting outside my apartment.

Charlotte's mouth fell open. "Excuse me? Sitting outside? Oh, this man is crazy."

Marie smirked. "Girl, I ran up and hugged him, and kissed him too."

"Really Marie," I hope you didn't mess that dinner date up.

"I know, Char! But no, of course, I didn't. It's Dupree though! I told him I had somewhere to go, so I had to hurry into the house, but it was good to see him."

"He was acting all chill, like, okay, I see you got somewhere to go. That's cool. Just make sure you call me when you're done."

"I said ok, and I went into the house to get dressed for my date. I could not wait.

"Terrence picked me up, opened my door, and treated me like a queen. I wasn't expecting it at all. I played it cool, but inside? I was wowed!"

Charlotte yelled. "Yesss! Girl, that's how it's supposed to be! But you already know, most men these days don't move like that."

Marie sighed dreamily. "Exactly! But Char, this man? He's different. He moves like a real man. Everything he did was so effortless and so natural like he was just born to lead. And baby, I fell in line with no hesitation. He took me to this fancy steakhouse downtown. I had never even heard of it! The food? Immaculate. The vibe? So smooth. I felt like I was being catered to the whole night."

Charlotte smiled. "Amazing, I love this for you! What's the name of the restaurant?"

Marie waved Charlotte's question off. "Something fancy, I don't even remember. You know I don't be out here eating steak like that! But everything was top-tier, clean, classy, and just perfect."

Charlotte sighed happily. "Wow, Marie. This sounds like a whole experience."

"Oh, it was," Marie said. "But listen to this, Terrence wasn't just there to impress me with dinner. He was asking me real questions, Char. Like, what do you do? What are your goals? Where do you see yourself in the future? And girl, it threw me! I actually had to think. It took me back to college, when my professor told us about how she had all these dreams but never chased them because life got in the way. I realized, I don't want to be like that. I love my job at Bergan Mercy, but I've always wanted my own practice. Not for fame, not for a name, but for the people. I want to create a space where my clients feel safe. You know like not worried about who might see them or what people might think."

Charlotte gasped. "Girl, I can hear it in your voice. That night did something to you."

Marie nodded, smiling. "It did. And get this, since he's an investor, he actually invests in businesses like mine. He was like, if this is something you want to do, I might be able to help you build it. Just like that! No strings, no weird energy. Just straight support."

Charlotte nearly dropped her phone. "Wait what? He really said that?"

Marie laughed. "Yes! I was shaken. It made me realize I've been thinking too small! Like, girl, I need to level all the way up."

Charlotte was practically screaming. "Marie, do you understand what is happening right now?! You just met a real man. Not some basic, half-stepping dude. A real one! Girl, I've been looking for a real man like that since I knew I liked men, and I ain't never found one! I need to know if he has any friends because whew."

Marie and Charlotte burst into laughter.

Marie sighed, still glowing. "Girl, and the way we talked, it wasn't just small talk. We laughed, we vibed, we were just in sync. It felt so easy. And it made me want more for myself. Like, I'm good, but I want to be great. And he made me realize I've been holding myself back."

Charlotte exhaled deeply. "Marie, I am so happy for you."

"Girl, me too. Thank you. Then, after that queen treatment I just got, all that happiness, and that high I was on from my date, I still called Dupree."

Charlotte groaned. "Marie!"

"I know, and I was totally let down by what happened next," Marie exclaimed.

"I hope it was not the same thing that happened last time?" Charlotte said with disappointment in her voice.

"Yes, the same old stuff, Charlotte." I was so upset and pissed off."

Charlotte groaned louder. "Nooo, Marie! So, Dupree was on the phone with some girl talking loudly on purpose?"

Marie rolled her eyes. "Of course. She was in the background, being extra, talking crazy. And I knew she wanted me to hear her. But you know what? A real woman would shut up the second she heard her man on the phone with another woman, especially me. But she was doing the most, so I let Dupree have it. I told him straight up this was the last time. If he keeps playing,

I'm done. Because after what I had just experienced? That disrespect was trash."

Charlotte clapped. "Oh, I felt that! That's right! Men can be so stupid. Dupree loves you for sure, but he does not know how to handle you. Please tell me you didn't go see him."

Marie hesitated.

Charlotte gasped. "Marie."

Marie giggled. "Yes, I still went to see my baby."

Charlotte groaned again. "Girl! That man does not deserve you after all that foolishness!"

Marie sighed. "I know, Char. But I needed all that greatness in my life last night."

Charlotte huffed. "I get it. I just hate when a man has us like this; wrapped up, even when we know better."

Marie nodded. "I swear, Char, Ima do better next time."

Both of them burst into laughter.

Marie suddenly perked up. "Okay, Char, I just pulled up to Charie's Sunshine Cafe, and, I see my king."

Charlotte gasped. "Not king!"

Marie grinned. "King, Girl. Because he treats me like a queen. He treats me better than my daddy does, and you know my daddy always told me, 'A man should treat you better than I do.'"

Charlotte sucked her teeth. "Well, dang!"

Marie nodded. "Yeah, I know. And I'm really hoping this is Terrence's real energy and not just his representative."

Charlotte hummed. "Mmm. We shall see."

Marie laughed. "Alright, Girl, I'll call you later."

"Alright, love you, Cuzzo."

"Love you too."

After Marie hung up her phone, she sat in her car, watching Terrence walk toward her, as she waited for her door to be opened so she could get out.

Chapter Eighteen

"Good morning, Beautiful," Terrence said, checking Marie out.

Marie stepped out of her car, and Terrence closed the door behind her. His deep voice carried warmth, and his eyes filled with admiration as they lingered on her.

"You look amazing, Beautiful. That blue looks fabulous on you," Terrence said, his smile was easy and sincere.

Marie beamed. "Oh, thank you so much, Terrence. I really appreciate that. And let me just say, this chocolate brown on you is perfect. You love that Adidas, I swear," Marie teased. "And you smell so good."

"You do too," Terrence replied, leaning in for a hug that lasted just a second longer than necessary. Their chemistry was undeniable.

They walked side by side into Charie's Sunshine Cafe, where the warmth of the morning sun cast a soft glow through the windows.

The hostess greeted them and led them to a cozy booth by the window. As they settled in, Terrence looked across the table. His eyes were locked on Marie.

"How are you today, Beautiful?"

Marie exhaled, her smile genuine, "I'm doing great. And you?"

"Better now," Terrence said smoothly. "It's always great to see you. Thank you for accepting my invitation. So, what's been going on?"

"Not much," Marie admitted.

The waitress arrived, taking their drink orders before slipping away.

Marie turned the question back on Terrence. "How about you?"

"I've been focused on some investments I have pending. I'm just trying to get things in place, but really, not much. Heading back home today, so I'm glad I got to see you one last time before I go."

Marie tilted her head. "You know, I never did ask, where are you from?"

Terrence chuckled. "Funny, right? You never asked, and I never told you. I'm from Mississippi. Jackson, to be exact. Ever heard of it?

The waitress returned with their drinks and took their order.

Marie sipped her orange juice, "Of course, I've heard of Mississippi, but I don't know much about

Jackson. Is it country? I mean, honestly, when I hear about Mississippi, it's usually about racism. Is it really that bad?"

Terrence met Marie's gaze, his expression serious. "Some parts, yeah. Mississippi has a history, no doubt. But Jackson? Jackson is different. Sure, racism exists, but our Black community is strong. We own businesses, and we thrive. We have Black millionaires. We work hard, we are educated, and we build wealth. We teach our kids to do the same."

Marie nodded, impressed. "Wow. I didn't know that. That's really interesting."

Terrence leaned in slightly. "You'll have to come visit me one day."

Marie raised a brow. "Wait. You want me to come to Jackson?"

"Of course," Terrence said, flashing that easy smile again. "I'd love for you to see where I'm from. I'll take you around, show you the city, introduce you to some good people, and we'll eat some really good food. Trust me, you'll have a great time."

Marie hesitated, then laughed. "I mean I can I do that? I do like to travel, and I don't have to stay long. Maybe a couple of days. I make my own schedule at work, so it is possible."

"Perfect," Terrence said. "Let's set a date. What works for you? Maybe a weekend?

Marie thought for a moment. "Actually, in three weeks, I have a few days off. I like taking Saturday through Monday instead of Friday through Sunday. It just works better for me."

"Alright then," Terrence said decisively. "We're making this happen. I'll get your ticket, book your hotel, and we will lock it in today. No need to wait."

Just then, their food arrived hot, fresh, and beautifully plated.

Marie's eyes widened. "Wow. This looks amazing, and you've got me speechless."

Terrence grinned. "Speechless?"

Marie blushed slightly, then smiled. "Yeah, and that's rare for me to be speechcless." She looked at Terrence. "You are consistent. Your words and your energy seem like the real you."

"It is the real me," Terrence said simply.

Marie held his gaze. "See, I say that because sometimes people send their representative first. They start out charming, saying all the right things, but eventually, they change. They turn into someone who belittles you and makes you feel small. I've seen it happen too many times."

Terrence's expression turned serious. "I don't know who hurt you like that, but let me be clear, I am not him. I am Terrence Marquice. Who I am now is who I am, period. And if you ever feel something is off, I need you to tell me. If I'm wrong about something, I want to fix it.

Marie sat back, stunned. "Terrence, I am not use to this. I am not use to a man, besides my dad, caring about how I feel, or a man making sure I am comfortable, or that I am heard. I am use to staying quiet or fighting for respect. But you, you do this naturally. And it baffles me."

Terrence reached for his coffee, taking a slow sip before setting it down. "This is me." He met Marie's eyes again. "And if nothing else, we can be lifelong friends. That's what I'm here for."

Marie and Terrence continued eating their meal, laughing and talking as the conversation flowed effortlessly.

Before they left, Terrence casually asked, "Who do you fly with? Where do you like to stay?"

Marie rattled off her preferences, and to her surprise, Terrence pulled out his phone and booked her flight with Delta and a room at the Hilton Garden Inn.

"And just so we're clear," Terrence added, his tone firm yet reassuring, "I booked your room. I have my own house, and that's where I'll be. Just because you're coming for me doesn't mean we have to stay together. You don't owe me anything."

Marie exhaled. "That is exactly what I was thinking. I mean, I don't even really know you, but I do know you."

Terrence nodded. "Exactly. But we will get to know each other. And I promise, I'm not looking for anything. Let's just see where this goes. I believe in divine connections."

Marie shook her head slightly, still stunned. "Me too, now."

They finished their meal, and Terrence paid the tab, leaving a generous tip. As they stepped outside, as usual, he opened Marie's car door for her.

Their eyes met one last time and they hugged, before Marie slid into the driver's seat.

"Drive safe, Beautiful," Terrence said softly.

"Thank you, Terrence," Marie replied, her voice just above a whisper.

As she pulled away, Marie couldn't shake the feeling that something had just shifted. Something real. Something different. And maybe, just maybe, something divine.

Chapter Nineteen

Marie and Catherine had talked earlier in the week and planned to meet Sunday evening to discuss how Catherine would tell Dakar about the new baby. That evening, Catherine called to let Marie know she was on her way.

"Alright, cool, see you soon," Marie said before hanging up.

A few minutes later, the doorbell rang. Marie went down and let Catherine in. When she stepped inside, they hugged warmly.

"Hey, Marie! Mmm, it smells so good in here. Gosh, I just love the way your house always smells," Catherine said, taking a deep breath.

Marie grinned. "You already know! I stay stocked up on my plug-ins."

Catherine laughed. "Oh, I know, Girl!"

They sat down, and Marie got straight to the point. "So, what's the plan? How do you want to tell Dakar? Do you want to make it a big surprise or something intimate? You know I got ideas for days. So just tell me what you want, and I will make it happen."

Catherine sighed. "Okay, so his birthday is in about five weeks. I was thinking of planning a small dinner for just a couple of his close friends, me, and you, and maybe Tasha and Brielle, if they can make it. Something simple but meaningful."

Marie nodded. "I love that idea. Where do you want to have it? What is Dakar's favorite spot?"

"You know he loves Carter's Café," Catherine said. "What if we just keep it casual and do a burger night there?"

Marie smiled. "Perfect. Carter's Café it is. Here's what we'll do. I'll get some decorations for the table to set the birthday vibe. You get him a gift, but instead of something traditional, make it baby-themed, like a gift bag with tiny socks, a onesie, little gloves, and a baby hat. And you wear a shirt that says, Happy Birthday, I Love You, and We're Having a Baby!"

Catherine gasped. "Oh my God, Marie! That is so cute and fun! I love it. Honestly, I think Dakar would love it too. I've been stressing over how to tell him, but this feels right."

Marie nodded confidently. "Oh yeah, he's gonna be so happy."

Catherine exhaled. "Good, because we need to do this soon. I made a doctor's appointment for the Wednesday after his birthday. So, I want this to be a moment we can both enjoy before we start all the prenatal stuff."

"Got it. I'll call Fuddruckers tomorrow to see if we need reservations or if we can just walk in," Marie assured Catherine.

Catherine smiled. "I'm so excited. But enough about me, what's been going on with you? I know I've been a little distant. I've just had so much on my mind. But I'm really embracing this baby now. I swear, I think I felt my stomach move, even though I know it's early. The doctor says I'm about 14 weeks, which is crazy because I was still getting my period! That's why I need that appointment."

Marie nodded knowingly. "Girl, it's okay. You know how we do. We get caught up in life, then pick right back up like no time has passed. You were not being distant. We're best friends; we just roll like that."

Catherine sighed, relieved. "Thanks, Marie. It really has been overwhelming. But you know what we need? A girl's happy hour! Me, you, Tasha, and Brielle. We haven't all hung out in forever."

Marie grinned. "Agreed! I'll set it up. This is the third time I have said it. I am calling everyone with the date tomorrow. I am looking at a Tuesday."

Catherine groaned. "Any Tuesday after 5:00 PM works for me. You already know. Marie, listen though. We are not going to Grown Folks Lounge again!"

Marie gasped, pretending to be offended. "Excuse me! You know their food is good!"

I'm not saying their food is not good," Catherine laughed. "I'm just saying we always end up there when you pick!"

Marie shrugged. "And for good reason! We all like it; we always know what we want, and we don't have to spend three days arguing over where to go!"

Catherine laughed. "Fine, fine. But seriously, we need this."

"And speaking of catching up," Marie said, Girl, you will not believe this, I met someone."

Catherine's eyes widened. "Wait, what? Who?"

Marie smirked. "His name is Terrence. And, Honey, he is a man."

Catherine gasped. "Wait, wait, hold up. What about Dupree?"

Marie rolled her eyes playfully. Dupree is Dupree. He's not going anywhere, but listen, Terrence is different. Grown. Mature. He moves like a man who knows what he wants."

Catherine shook her head. "And Marcellus?"

Marie laughed. "Girl, Marcellus is still Marcellus. I swear, him and Dupree are always gonna be a part of my story."

Catherine smirked. "Until one day, all three of y'all cross paths!"

Marie giggled. "And if that happens? No drama. I'd introduce them and keep it moving. I never want my relationships to turn into a mess. But trust me, they both know I'm not exclusive to them. I keep it real with them. They, on the other hand? They sneak around. And that's fine, but I don't have to sneak. I tell the truth, so they can't ever say I played them."

Catherine shook her head, laughing. "Girl, you are something else."

Marie smirked. "But listen! Terrence is from Jackson, Mississippi. And guess what? In three weeks, I'm going down there to see him!"

Catherine's jaw dropped. "What? You're going to Jackson, Mississippi, for a man?"

Marie laughed. "Yes! I am going to Mississippi, but no, I am not going for a man. I am going to see a man who invited me to his city. There is a difference. Terrence is an investor; he's 35, and let me tell you, he moves differently. No drama and no mess, just a grown man who knows what he wants."

Catherine let out a deep sigh. "Wow. You got yourself a mature man."

Marie nodded. "Exactly."

Marie and Catherine talked for hours. Eventually, they went to the kitchen and made turkey and cheese sandwiches with chips and soda. The conversation flowed effortlessly, catching up on everything from Catherine's pregnancy to Marie's tangled love life.

It wasn't until after 10:00 PM that Catherine finally decided to leave. As they walked outside, Catherine shook her head with a smirk. Girl, I still can't believe you're going to Mississippi with some man.

Marie grinned. "Believe it, Baby! A girl's gotta explore her options!"

Marie and Catherine hugged tightly before Catherine got in her car and drove off. Marie walked back inside, her heart full, her mind racing with everything that was unfolding in her life.

One thing was for sure, change was coming. And Marie was ready for it.

Chapter Twenty

Marie squinted at the clock. 6:47 a.m. "Who in the world would be ringing my doorbell this early?" She groaned, tightening the belt on her robe as she shuffled toward the door. The doorbell rang again, more insistent this time.

"Who is it?" Marie questioned.

A familiar but unwelcomed voice came through the door. "It's Vanessa. I need to talk to you."

Marie froze, then scoffed to herself. "Vanessa? At my apartment?" She rolled her eyes, walked down and unlocked the door, but then stepped outside instead of inviting Vanessa in. The morning air hit her bare legs, but she ignored it, folding her arms. "Excuse me, what are you doing at my apartment?" Marie demanded.

Vanessa stood on the front step with her arms crossed and an expectant look on her face. "I came to get Marcellus. I know he is here."

Marie blinked, then let out a short, disbelieving laugh. "Oh, is that right? So, you just figured you would show up at my door at the crack of dawn, thinking you would catch Marcellus here?"

Vanessa's expression didn't waver. "Well, yeah. He's in town, and let's be honest. Y'all always have something going on."

Marie exhaled sharply, already exhausted by the conversation. "First of all, I didn't even know Marcellus was in town. Second, I haven't talked to him. Third, what makes you think he'd be here with me?"

Vanessa rolled her eyes. "Please. I know how you all are, and I wanted to let you know that we are having issues again."

Marie gave Vanessa a slow, unimpressed blink. "Oh, you don't say?" She said dryly. "The same man you've been trashing? The same one you said was broke and from the projects and just using you for your money? That man? And yet here you are, hunting him down like a lost puppy."

Vanessa's lips smacked loudly. "Don't act like you don't know how Marcellus is. He's always got some girl on the side, always lying, always needing something!"

"Stop right there!" Marie's voice was sharp, cutting through Vanessa's rant. She stepped closer, her eyes locked onto Vanessa's.

Vanessa hesitated and shifted her weight.

"First of all," Marie continued, "Marcellus is my best friend. And unlike you, I don't and never will sit around dragging his name through the dirt while claiming to love him. You said he was your man, right? So, keep that same energy. He's your problem, not mine."

Vanessa scoffed. "You always defend him."

"Because I actually respect Marcellus, unlike you," Marie said in a firm voice. "You don't get to talk down on my best friend. You don't get to throw everything you have done for Marcellus in his face and then talk about him. That's not love, Vanessa. That's control."

Vanessa's mouth opened, then closed. She looked away for a moment before muttering, "Well, we are working on things. We are actually trying to have a baby."

Marie stared at Vanessa for a long moment. Then, she let out a slow, dramatic blink before bursting into laughter, not out of humor, but disbelief. "Oh, so let me get this straight." Marie folded her arms. "You showed up at my door, talking about how terrible Marcellus is, how he is always cheating, always broke, always a problem. And now you're telling me y'all are trying to bring a whole baby into this mess? Girl, do you even hear yourself? You are reaching, and I am laughing at you on the inside."

Vanessa's face flushed. "I just thought you should know."

Marie held up a hand, cutting Vanessa off. "No. You thought wrong!" Marie's voice was ice. "You came to my house fishing for answers, hoping to catch Marcellus slipping. But here is the truth: I haven't seen Marcellus, and I don't know what he is doing. Honestly, I don't care. And neither should you, if you were really about what you say.

Vanessa's lips pressed into a thin line.

Marie took a step forward, lowering her voice but making sure every word hit its mark. "Now let me be crystal clear, Vanessa. You do not get to show up at my home, uninvited, running your mouth about Marcellus. You don't get to ring my doorbell, demanding conversations you have no business having. We are not friends, Vanessa. So don't knock on my door or ring my doorbell ever again."

Marie turned toward her apartment, tossing one final warning over her shoulder.

"Now, get away from my doorstep before I remove you."

Vanessa glared but said nothing. She spun on her heel and stomped off, getting into a sleek black rental car.

Marie exhaled, shaking her head as she locked the door behind herself. "Some people never learn."

Chapter Twenty-One

Do you see how my morning just started? I am still trying to process the level of disrespect I had to deal with.

It's early, way too early for anybody to be ringing my doorbell, right? I'm minding my business, sleeping peacefully, when my doorbell starts ringing like somebody's life depends on it. I'm thinking, who in the world? Now, let's pause right there. What would have possessed this girl to show up at my house? We are not friends. We are not cool. And let's be real, she had zero business being here. But here she is, early in the morning, looking for Marcellus like he's lost or something. Talking about, I know he's here.

Girl, what? I shut that down real quick. I let her know she didn't belong at my apartment, she had no reason to be on my doorstep, and she most definitely wasn't coming inside. The audacity!

I did not call Marcellus after that. One thing about me? I already knew if he was in town, he was going to reach out to me. And sure enough, about an hour later, my phone rang.

He was all happy, all excited, talking about, I'm in town! I'll be here for four days, we gotta hang out. And I'm like, yeah, about that.

I had to tell him the news. I said, "So, your little delusional, wanna-be girlfriend came banging on my doorstep this morning, talking about you."

And do you know what Marcellus said? "He said, I didn't even tell her I was coming! She must have looked it up!"

Exactly. Because the girl is obsessed.

Then he goes, "Yeah, we're on the outs, but then again, we're always on the outs. We were only ever in when we first met."

I just shook my head. Same story, different day.

He starts telling me, "Man, she doesn't get it. I've told her I'm done, I've told her I want to move on, but she won't let go. She treats me like trash, talks to me crazy, and get this she's even called me the N-word before, twice."

"Excuse me, what?" I questioned loudly. Oh, it took everything in me to stay calm. But Marcellus, he already knows. We all know. Vanessa is rude, disrespectful, and on top of that, jealous. She really thinks she can control him just because her family has money.

But here's the part that really got me. Marcellus tells me, I'm about to sit down with her dad and let him know exactly how she's been treating me. I'm gonna thank him for everything he's done, let him know I appreciate it, and if I owe him anything, I'll pay him back. Because I was never using them. They looked out for me, and I respect that. But his daughter? No. I can't do it anymore.

And honestly? I was proud of him. Because it is about time.

But then he hit me with something even bigger.

He said, "Oh, and nobody knows this yet, but I just signed a new contract with a new team. I left early last night to handle everything. This time, this is my money. Nobody else's. I don't owe anybody anything. And now, I can take care of myself and my family without anyone hanging it over my head."

And let me tell you I love that for him. He deserves it. No more people acting like they own him. No more Vanessa throwing money in his face. He's free.

And then, just to really set things straight, he tells me, and by the way, I don't know what Vanessa told you, but I have made it very clear I do not want a baby with her. That is not happening.

Oh, I had to laugh. Because y'all, didnt she just tell me they were trying to have a baby? That they were hoping it would happen? Oh my!

So, I told him straight up, "Oh yeah," she told me. She said, "You were working on it, talking all this extra nonsense. But honestly, she was so all over the place that I knew she was just fishing for information."

And I made sure to remind him that I checked her. I let her know she was way out of line showing up at my house like that. I told her, Don't ever come back here again. And if you don't leave now, I will remove you.

And trust me she got the message.

I told Marcellus, "She should already know never to come my way again. But just in case she forgot? I made it real clear."

And that's that.

So yeah, y'all. Vanessa is delusional. But guess what? Marcellus is done playing her game. And I am done entertaining her nonsense.

Moral of the story? Know your place. And don't come knocking where you are not welcome.

Chapter Twenty-Two

"Okay, so for happy hour," Marie said, with her phone tucked between her ear and shoulder, "we can either do this Tuesday or the following Tuesday. I'm cool with whatever."

"I'm flexible too," Catherine replied. "Let's see what everybody else is working with."

"Alright," Marie said. "Let's click over and get Tasha, then one of us can call Brielle."

Catherine clicked over.

"Hello?"

"Hey, Tash," Catherine said. "It's me. Marie's on the line too."

"Hey, y'all," Tasha said. "What's up?"

"We're just checking in," Marie added, "seeing how you're doing, and trying to lock in this happy hour."

"Ooo, finally," Tasha laughed. "Hold on one second though, I gotta hang up with my mom."

"No problem."

A moment later, Tasha clicked back in.

"Okay, I'm back. Let me call Brielle." She clicked over again.

"Hello?"

"Hey, Brielle," Tasha said. "It's me, Marie and Catherine are on too."

"Well, hey, hey, hey," Brielle said. "Look at us with the three-way call."

"Right," Catherine laughed. "It's time."

"So, here's the deal," Marie said. "We're trying to set up happy hour. How does Tuesday sound?"

"This Tuesday or next?" Brielle asked.

"Next Tuesday works for me," Catherine said.

"Same," Marie added.

"Next Tuesday is good," Tasha said.

"Okay, next Tuesday it is," Brielle confirmed. "What time?"

"Six o'clock?" Catherine suggested.

"Six works for me," Marie said.

"Perfect," Tasha said.

"Six is good," Brielle agreed. "So, where we going?"

"Honestly," Marie said, "let's just go to Grown Folks Lounge. We don't need to reinvent the wheel."

"Exactly," Catherine said. "G always takes care of us."

"And we already know the food is good," Tasha added. "We can try a new spot another day, like a Saturday when we're not rushing."

"That makes sense," Brielle said. "I'm in."

"So, it's settled," Tasha said. "Next Tuesday, six o'clock, Grown Folks Lounge."

"Look at us," Marie smiled. "Things are lining up."

"My week's been good," Catherine said.

"Mine too," Brielle added.

"Same here," Tasha said.

"Well, I love y'all," Marie said. "I can't wait."

"Love you too," Tasha said.

"Love y'all," Brielle said.

"Always," Catherine added.

They said their goodbyes and hung up, smiling, grateful, and excited.

Chapter Twenty-Three

"Hey, Marie! How are you doing, daughter?"

"I'm doing good, Mom."

"Okay, what's up?"

"I was wondering if I could come by and see you. I haven't seen or talked to you in a little while, which is crazy because we usually talk almost every day."

Marie heard a slight hesitation before her mother replied, "I've got company, but you can come on by."

"Company? You don't even do company. Who's at your house?"

"Come on by; it's fine. You can talk to them too. You won't mind."

§§§§§§§§§§§§§§§§

Curiously, Marie grabbed her keys and headed to her mom's house. Using her key, she let herself in and walked into the living room. She gasped at the sight before her.

"Dad? Hi! What is going on here?" Marie asked, her face a mix of surprise and confusion.

Her father grinned. "What do you mean, what's going on? I'm visiting with your mom."

Marie shook her head, trying to process the scene. "I don't think it's funny, but okay. It's cool you guys are sitting here together, watching TV. This hasn't happened since I was a teenager, so it's just weird."

Marie's parents exchanged amused glances but said nothing. Marie took a deep breath, deciding to focus on the reason for her visit.

"Okay, so Mom and Dad, since you're both here, I was really coming to talk to Mom, but ok, I wanted to tell you about someone I met. Even though I feel weird, I'm going to talk."

Marie's dad leaned forward; his curiosity was evident. "Okay, so who'd you meet? This must be somebody special because you haven't talked about a guy since years ago when you met Marcellus and told me you had a boyfriend."

Marie nodded with a small smile playing on her lips. "I know, I know. So, I met a guy. I was coming back home, at the airport, and I met him. He's 35 years old, and honestly, I thought he was a drug dealer because of how he looked. He had on a Kangol hat and an Adidas tracksuit, and I just assumed. But when we started talking, I found out he's an investor. He has a daughter in the Air Force, which is why he was here visiting. He was once in the military himself, lives in Mississippi, and owns a business. He's an entrepreneur and a genuinely nice guy. He was such a gentleman. Everything he did was so manly. It was almost like, this is the type of man you would want me to be with, Dad. He acts just like you, Dad. He's very kind and friendly. I'm just not used to meeting guys like this."

Marie's mom chimed in, "Okay, so he's 35, a business owner, nice guy, and was here to visit his daughter. It all sounds good. Does he have a wife?"

Marie paused with realization dawning. "I never asked if he was married. I've never asked anyone that before. I don't know any married guys, so it didn't even cross my mind."

Her mom raised an eyebrow. "That's something you should consider. Did you see a ring on his finger?"

"I didn't even look," Marie admitted. "Nothing's ever told me to look or expect someone might be married."

Her dad nodded thoughtfully. "Sometimes, you have to think about stuff like that. He could be married, but it doesn't mean he is just because he's nice."

"True," her mom added. "I'm just saying, you're mentioning all these great things, and I'm thinking, let's make sure he's not married. He doesn't live here; you don't know much about him. When's he coming back?"

"That's the thing," Marie said. "I went out with him twice. The first time, he was all about me, asking questions and genuinely interested. He made me feel good; I was smiling a lot. I kept thinking, who is this guy? But again, he's like you, Dad. This is why I appreciate you for treating me so well because maybe I was in training to meet a man like this. Anyways, he invited me to visit him. He lives in Mississippi."

Her dad's brow furrowed. "Do you plan on going? You don't know anyone in Mississippi."

"Yes, I want to go. He said to come down, and I don't have to worry about anything. He's taking care of my plane ticket, which he has already done. He's booked my room and said he doesn't have to stay where I stay. He's not interested in that; he just wants me to see his town, where he's from, and show me around. He said it's my room, and I don't have to share it with him. He meant that."

Marie's mom smiled. "It sounds good; like a winner."

"Yeah, Mom, it sounds like a winner. I'm really intrigued and excited. I just want to see what he's about. I've never experienced this before, so I'm wondering, have I been choosing wrong, or is God trying to show me something better?"

Her dad chuckled. "When you start talking about God, you know it's something better."

"Yeah," Marie agreed. "It's like when I used to go to church, and they'd say this is a God thing. I felt like that the whole time; this has got to be God trying to show me something better because of what I've been going through."

Her dad's expression turned serious. "And what exactly have you been going through?"

"Well, you know, Marcellus and I are still cool."

"You two will always gonna be cool," her dad interjected. "You said you were best friends, right? And he's in the NFL now, doing great. Why wouldn't you be friends?"

"It's a lot, Dad. He has this girl who's always starting trouble, talking trash. It's just a lot. I want to be his friend and support him, but I don't want to deal with her. Then I have another friend, and we're cool, but it ends up being so much."

Marie's mom sighed. "Honestly, this sounds like me and your dad; the reason we ended up splitting up after all our years together, after all our understanding and love. It wasn't something we discussed with you. You didn't hear us arguing because we didn't want you to know. We wanted you to see that we were still friends, even though deep down, we probably had a secret resentment toward each other. But the love we had was stronger.

Your dad was out there; everyone knew him. He was making his way in life, making money, doing his thing, and he had all these girls around him. They knew he had me, but they were always in his face. It bothered me, and he acted like it was nothing. The one time another guy talks to me, and I'm doing exactly what your dad is doing, talking to other people and enjoying the conversation, your dad leaves me. What is that?"

"Wait, what? Mom, so was Dad cheating on you?"

"He did."

"What?"

"It's a long story," her dad explained.

"And you stuck with him?"

"I did, and there was almost a child that came out of that cheating, but thank God they lost it."

"Wow, Mom, heck no. I mean that in the most respectful way, but I would not have been able to handle that. So, did you cheat too, Mom?"

"Mentally, yes, but physically, no."

"Mentally?"

"Yes, I was mentally attached to Lewis. He was smart, easy to talk to, and he said all the right things. He was such a man and had so much love and respect for me."

"Wow, sounds like Terrence."

"Oh, okay, Terrence is his name," Marie's dad said. "He and Lewis get on my nerves."

They all laughed.

"Anyways, so what happened? I'm confused," Marie said.

"I didn't like that your mom was with another man," Marie's dad admitted. "I thought they were together, mentally and physically. I didn't know. But I saw your mom and Lewis all hugged up at a restaurant, sitting beside each other, not across. She was laughing and smiling; to me, she seemed too happy to be just mentally connected. I couldn't get past it. I was hurt, pissed off, embarrassed because my guys were with me, and I was done."

"Wow, just like that?"

"Just like that," Marie's mother confirmed. "Your dad knew how much I loved him, but I had been mentally divorced for a couple of years. So, we walked away, appearing cool to others but with a secret resentment toward each other. For the sake of family and your well-being, we always showed major love to one another."

"Wow," Marie said. "So, since we're on the topic, what are you doing at Mom's house, Dad? I've only known y'all to be best friends since the divorce, but I've never seen you here without me."

"Well," Marie's dad said, glancing at Marie's mom, "You want me to fill her in?"

Elaine blushed and smiled. "You might as well," she said.

"Well, Princess," Marie's dad began, "Me and your mom have been dating for about four months."

Marie's smile widened, and she blinked in surprise. "Really? That's amazing. I've always hoped you'd find your way back to each other."

Her mom reached out, squeezing her hand. "Life has a way of bringing us full circle."

Marie smiled, feeling a warmth between her parents that she hadn't felt in years. "I'm so happy for you both."

As she prepared to leave, Marie's dad hugged her tightly. "Remember, follow your heart, Princess, and always ask the important questions."

"I will, Dad. I love you both. Marie suddenly leaned over, clutching her chest. "Ouch!" she gasped.

Her dad sprang forward, alarmed. "Wait! What? Are you okay, Princess? You're holding your chest."

Marie winced, struggling to speak. "I, I don't know. This is the second time it's happened. My right arm is hurting too. And now my shoulder, it just gave out. Oh my God."

Her mother stood up quickly, her voice sharp with concern. "Marie, what do you mean this is the second time? And you haven't gone to get it checked?"

"No, ma'am, I haven't," Marie admitted, lowering her eyes. "You're right. I should've, I just…"

"You work at a hospital!" Marie's mom cut her off. "You're a therapist, for God's sake. Why are you ignoring chest pain? Are you trying to have a heart attack?"

"I know, Mom, I know. I'm sorry. I'm really sorry."

Marie's dad tried to step in gently. "Hey, hey, don't stress her out. She's clearly in pain. We need to focus on getting her help, not piling on."

Her mom pressed on. "I'm not trying to stress her. I'm trying to save her life. Chest pain and arm pain? Girl, you know what that can mean. You need to be seen by a doctor tonight, Marie."

"I'll go in the morning, okay? It's letting up now." Marie took a breath, but winced again. "It's just that every time I breathe in, it feels like a sharp, stabbing pain."

"And your right arm is hurting too?" her mom asked sarcastically.

Marie nodded. "Yes, ma'am.

Her mother looked at her husband. "That's not good. Isn't that a warning sign of a heart attack or stroke?"

Marie quickly answered, "It can be, but it doesn't always mean that's what's happening. I can still move my fingers, and make a fist, see? I don't feel numb, but yeah I'll go. I'm not trying to die in my sleep, trust me."

Her dad stepped forward, placing a hand on her shoulder. "Princess, don't play tough. This isn't about strength. Real strength is knowing when something's wrong and doing something about it. Pain is your body's warning, don't ignore it."

"Okay, Dad. I hear you," Marie said softly, rubbing her chest one last time. She hugged her parents, forcing a smile, then turned and walked toward the door.

As it closed behind her, her mother sighed. "I don't get it. Why would she just live with chest pain? She knows better."

"I know," her father replied. "It doesn't make sense. She can't be afraid of doctors, she is one, in a sense. Maybe she's scared, but still…"

"I just don't want to lose my baby," her mother whispered.

"Me either," her dad said, his voice heavy.

They stood in silence as Marie drove away into the night.

Chapter Twenty-Four

As I drove away, I could still hear my parents'
voices echoing in my head. You're a nurse! You know
better! Don't play tough! They weren't wrong. But the
truth is, this pain? It's not just physical. It's emotional.
Mental. Spiritual. And I've been carrying it for so long
that I don't even know what normal feels like anymore.

I didn't go get checked because I've been trying
to convince myself that everything is fine. Because when
you're the strong one, when people always look to you
for answers, for comfort, and for direction, you don't
get to break. You don't get to fall apart. You just keep
going, even when your chest is screaming, and your
spirit is tired.

But tonight hit different. The look in my parents'
eyes scared me. Not because they were angry, but
because they were scared. Because they saw something
in me, I've been ignoring. I felt that pain shoot through
my chest and down my arm, and for a moment, I really
did wonder if this was it. If this was the night my body
would finally say enough is enough.

I know all the signs. I've taught people about
them. Cared for patients who ignored them. Buried a

few who waited too long. And yet here I am, doing the same thing.

Why?

Maybe because part of me still doesn't feel seen. Perhaps because I've been carrying so much pain from the past, responsibilities in the present, and pressure about the future. Maybe because I've mastered looking okay when I'm not. But that's not strength. That's survival. And tonight, I realized, I don't want to just survive anymore. I want to live, really live. I want to breathe without fear, feel without guilt, and rest without worry.

Chapter Twenty-Five

I'm truly happy for my parents. As I head home, I keep thinking about it. They are getting back together.

It's amazing, really. Sitting there with them, feeling their energy, watching them laugh, seeing that old familiar closeness takes me back, back to when I was a kid, watching my parents be so in love. They were always hugging, always kissing, always laughing. I used to dream of growing up and having that kind of love for myself. I wanted a family, but bigger. And I wanted my husband to be just like my dad.

But then, when I was around twelve, everything changed. I came home from school one day, and my parents were both sitting at the table. The air felt different; heavy. My dad looked at me and said, Marie, I hate to talk to you like this. I don't want you to feel the pain of our mistakes, but your mom and I are splitting up. I'm moving out.

I sat there frozen, nodding, but inside, my heart was crying. I wanted to scream, no, no, no. This isn't right. This isn't happening. But I just sat there.

My mom chimed in, we still love each other. We are still best friends. This is just what is best for us.

I wanted to believe them. I wanted to believe that we were still a family, that things wouldn't change, that love was still real. But at that moment, all I felt was loss.

See, I had friends who didn't have both parents at home. They used to tell me how lucky I was and how much they admired my family. They loved seeing my parents at my events, laughing together, and supporting me. To them, my parents were rare and special. And now I felt like I was about to become just like everybody else. A kid from a broken home. A kid without a dream.

But my parents did something unexpected. They kept showing up together. They never let the world see the cracks. At school events, at family gatherings, and to everyone else, we were still the perfect family. And for a while, I held on to that illusion. I let myself believe that if no one else knew, maybe it wasn't real. But when I got home, the silence screamed at me.

There were no more late-night laughs on the couch, no more hugs that made me feel like everything in the world was safe, and no more feeling whole. I cried. I cried a lot. Even after I graduated from high school, I still cried. No matter how much they tried to soften the blow, the truth remained: I lost something I thought would always be there.

And yet, now, now they're back together.

It's everything I ever wanted. It's a dream I have held in my heart since I was twelve. But as much as it makes me happy, it also takes me back. Back to that broken girl who didn't know how to grieve what she lost.

Looking back, I realize my parents were trying to protect me. In their own ways, they were teaching me how to navigate love. My dad showed me how a man should treat me and how I should never accept being disrespected or mistreated. My mom, on the other hand, warned me not to get played. Don't let your feelings lead you, she'd say. Be smart. Guard your heart.

At the time, I didn't understand it. But now, I see it. They were trying to keep me from repeating their mistakes. Trying to make sure I wouldn't accept what they had accepted. Trying to make sure I didn't end up sitting at a table, breaking my own child's heart with the same words they told me. And maybe that is why I became so guarded. Maybe that's why I'm so hardcore now.

Divorce changed me. It made me question love: whether it was real, whether it lasted, or whether it even mattered. I lived in a contradiction: we were broken, but we weren't. We were apart, but to the world, we were together. I never knew what was real and what was just a performance.

Now that they are back together, I can't help but wonder if it is healing. Or is this just a reminder of what was broken? Maybe it is both.

Maybe this is my sign to talk to God.

See, when I was younger, I had faith. I believed in God. But when things started falling apart, I questioned everything. If God is real, why would He let this happen?

But now, maybe He's showing me something. Maybe this full-circle moment isn't just about my parents finding their way back to each other. Maybe it's about me finding my way back, too. Maybe I needed to revisit this pain to see if I was really healed.

Chapter Twenty-Six

Upon arriving home, Marie decided to give Terrence a call. She needed to address the lingering question about his marital status before making any further plans.

"Hey, Terrence," Marie greeted him warmly when he answered.

"Hey there Beautiful! Great to hear from you. How's everything?" Terrence's voice was filled with genuine enthusiasm.

"Everything's good. I wanted to talk to you about something before my visit," Marie began, her tone serious yet gentle.

"Of course. What's on your mind Beautiful?" Terrence asked, sensing the importance of the conversation.

"I realized I never asked you this, but are you married, Terrence?" Marie's heart raced as she awaited his response.

There was a brief pause before Terrence replied, "No, I'm not married. I was, but my ex-wife and I divorced five years ago. It's just me and my girls.

Relief washed over Marie. "Thank you for being honest. I just needed to know before moving forward."

"I understand completely," Terrence said reassuringly. "I want us to be open with each other."

With that concern addressed, Marie felt more at ease about her upcoming trip.

Marie and Terrence sat on the phone talking for another hour before hanging up.

Chapter Twenty-Seven

The evening Marie and her friends had been waiting for had finally arrived.

Tuesday. Girls' happy hour. Six o'clock sharp at Grown Folks Lounge, where they always went when they wanted good food, good drinks, and grown conversation.

Brielle and Tasha arrived first. They grabbed a booth near the back, one of their usual spots, and immediately ordered waters for the table. After a brief debate, they settled on a fried mushroom appetizer to start.

Catherine arrived next, sliding into the booth with hugs all around. Marie was right behind her, coming in with her usual smile, relieved, honestly, to finally sit down with her girls.

The hugs were warm. The laughter was easy. For a moment, everything felt normal.

Drinks were ordered next. As usual, most of them ordered their favorite, Real LOVE Executive's Millionaire Moscato, the one they always joked tasted like celebration in a glass, but not Catherine.

"I'll just have cranberry juice on the rocks," she said casually.

Brielle raised an eyebrow. "Cranberry juice? On the rocks? Girl, what's going on? You not feeling good? Because cranberry juice usually means a yeast infection."

The table erupted in laughter.

"No," Catherine said, laughing too. "I'm fine. I just don't feel like drinking tonight. That's all."

Tasha clapped her hands together. "Alright then, what's everybody been up to? How's life?"

Catherine went first. "I'm good. Work was long, but I can't complain. I needed this tonight though."

"I'm good too," Brielle added. "Busy at work, but life is life. I'm just happy to see y'all."

"No complaints here either," Tasha said. "I'm good."

Marie nodded. "Life is good for me too," she said slowly. "But I do have some things I want to talk about. So don't act funny when I start talking."

Brielle sighed dramatically. "Here we go. What is it now, Marie?"

"Don't do that," Marie said. "I'm not starting anything."

Tasha jumped in. "Didn't we all come out to talk and have a good time?"

Catherine looked at Brielle. "Just because life is good doesn't mean nobody has anything going on. If Marie has something to say, she should be able to say it."

Brielle shrugged. "Whatever. Go ahead."

Marie hesitated, then took a breath. "Okay, well, my parents decided to get back together."

The table froze.

"What?" Brielle said.

"Are you serious?" Tasha asked.

"Oh, my goodness," Catherine whispered.

"Yes," Marie said. "After all these years. They've always been close, best friends really, but I found out recently that there were misunderstandings back then. My dad thought my mom was cheating. My mom thought my dad was cheating. Instead of talking, they just survived. For me."

Marie paused. "And tonight my mom called to tell me her and my dad went to the courthouse today and got remarried."

The table sat in stunned silence.

"That's a lot," Catherine said finally. "But honestly? That's beautiful."

Marie nodded. "It is. I'm not mad. It just brought up old emotions."

Before she could say more, a young waiter approached the table. "Hi, I'm Jeremy," he said with a smile. "I'll be taking care of y'all tonight. George told me y'all are regulars."

"That's our guy," Brielle said proudly.

Jeremy laughed. "I'm new. This is my second job. Are y'all ready to order?"

"Can you give us about ten minutes?" Marie asked.

"Of course," Jeremy said, walking away.

Brielle leaned forward. "Marie, you looked like you were flirting."

"I wasn't," Marie said.

"And even if she was?" Tasha snapped. "What is going on with you tonight?"

Marie hesitated again, then spoke. "There's also someone I met. His name is Terrence. He's from Jackson, Mississippi. He's a business owner, and he's really nice."

"That's amazing," Tasha said.

Brielle scoffed. "What about Dupree? Marcellus? You already got men."

Tasha's head snapped around. "Why are you being rude?"

"I'm just asking," Brielle said. "Why add another man?"

Marie stared at her. "I don't know what I did to you, Brielle, but something is wrong."

Jeremy came back. "Y'all ready?"

"Not yet," Marie said. Then, calmly, she turned to him. "How old are you?"

"Twenty-three."

"That's not bad. I'm twenty-seven," Marie smiled.

Brielle rolled her eyes. "Here we go again."

For Brielles's pleasure, Marie exchanged numbers with Jeremy and gave him a big hug. Then she asked, "Can you please give us a few more minutes?"

Then Marie turned to Brielle, pointing her finger in her face and said, "I didn't come here for this. I came to be with my friends. Brielle, you're being so disrespectful, and I don't understand why. I'm leaving," Tears blurred her vision as she walked out.

Brielle shook her head. "I wasn't trying to make her mad."

"You absolutely were," Catherine said. "That was rude."

Tasha stood. "I'm with Marie."

"So am I," Catherine said.

They left Brielle sitting alone; confused, defensive, and finally realizing something had gone very wrong.

Chapter Twenty-Eight

Marie let out a long breath. "Okay, what just happened?" she said out loud, her voice cracking a little. "Because that was not what I came out for. That was not it."

She stared straight ahead, blinking back tears.

"I didn't come to argue. I didn't come to compete. I didn't come to prove anything," she said, shaking her head. "I came to sit with my friends. I came to laugh. I came to share something good."

Her fingers tightened around the wheel. "And somehow, somehow it turned into that."

She scoffed softly. "I didn't say anything crazy. I didn't disrespect anybody. I didn't come in there acting brand new. So why did it feel like I was being checked? Like, I was being questioned? Like I needed permission to live my own life?"

Marie paused, swallowing hard. "Why did it feel like I wasn't safe at that table?"

The tears came then, slow and quiet. "That hurt," she whispered. "That really hurt."

She wiped her face with the back of her hand. "I don't understand it. I've always been me. I've always been real. I've always shown up. So why does it feel like the moment something good happens for me, the energy shifts?"

She laughed bitterly. "Is it because I'm happy? Is that it? Because I'm not complaining? Because I'm not settling like I used to?"

She shook her head again. "I didn't even get to finish what I was saying. I didn't even get to share."

Her voice softened. "My parents getting back together, that mattered to me. That brought up stuff I didn't even know I was still carrying. I just wanted my friends to hear me."

She leaned her head back against the seat. "And then Terrence," she said quietly. "I wasn't trying to show off. I wasn't trying to brag. I was just excited. I felt peaceful. I felt something different."

She sniffed. "And instead of being happy for me, it felt like I was being judged. Like I was doing too much. Like I needed to explain myself."

She exhaled slowly. "I'm tired of explaining myself."

She looked at her reflection in the rearview mirror. "I didn't walk out because I was mad," she said firmly. "I walked out because I was protecting myself. I wasn't about to sit there and let my feelings get stepped on."

"And you know what?" she added. "I don't regret leaving."

She nodded to herself. "I had a good day. A really good day. I'm not letting anyone take that from me. Not tonight. Not ever again."

Her shoulders relaxed just a little. "If something changed," Marie said softly, "then it changed. But I didn't change who I am."

She started the car. "And whoever can't handle that, that's not on me."

Marie pulled out of the parking lot, tears drying, heart still tender, but her spine straight.

She was hurt. But she was also clear.

Chapter Twenty-Nine

Brielle's Private Realization

Brielle sat alone at the booth long after everyone had left.

The fried mushrooms sat untouched. The table felt too big. Too quiet. She crossed her arms, annoyed at first. I wasn't even trying to be rude, she told herself. I was just asking questions. But the silence didn't agree with her.

Her eyes followed the empty space where Marie had been sitting. And for the first time that night, the truth crept in, not loud, not accusing, just honest.

Why did that bother me so much? Brielle sighed and leaned back. It wasn't about Terrence. It wasn't about Dupree or Marcellus. And it definitely wasn't about Jeremy.

It was about the glow. Marie had walked in different. Lighter. Softer. Happier. And Brielle had noticed it the moment she sat down. She's changing, Brielle thought. And I didn't like how it made me feel.

She picked at a napkin, jaw tightening. What if Marie really had found something better? What if she really was leveling up?

And what did that say about her? The sarcasm hadn't been accidental. It had been defense. "I messed that up," Brielle muttered under her breath.

She thought about how Marie always showed up. Always listened. Always gave grace. And tonight, Brielle had given none. The realization hit hard. I owe her an apology. But Brielle also knew something else. Apologies meant admitting fear. And fear meant admitting she wasn't as secure as she pretended to be.

She sat there until the waitress cleared the table, then finally stood. "This ain't over," she said quietly. "Not like this." But whether Marie would still be open when Brielle found the courage, that part, she didn't know.

Chapter Thirty

Marie's phone rang again. She didn't look at it this time. It had already been ringing on and off for the past hour. She knew who it was. She didn't need to check the screen to know. She laid the phone face down on the nightstand and exhaled.

"Not tonight," she whispered to herself.

She kicked off her shoes, changed into something comfortable, and sat on the edge of the bed. The silence felt loud at first, but she needed it.

"I just need tonight," she said softly. "Just one night to think. To feel. To be still." She wasn't angry anymore, just drained. She replayed the evening in her mind, not to torture herself, but to understand it. The tone. The looks. The little comments that weren't jokes. The way the air at the table shifted without warning.

"I didn't imagine that," she said quietly. "I know what I felt." Her phone rang again.

She picked it up this time, glanced at the screen, Catherine. Then another, Tasha. Then Brielle.

Marie locked the phone and set it back down.

"I don't want explanations," she said. "I don't want apologies tonight. I don't want to talk myself out of my feelings." She laid back, staring at the ceiling.

"For once, I'm choosing peace," she said. "And peace means quiet."

Chapter Thirty-One

The knock on the door was soft but familiar. Marie had just finished getting dressed for work when she heard it. She already knew who it was. She opened the door to find Catherine standing there with concern written all over her face.

"Hey," Catherine said gently. "I hope it's okay that I came by."

"It's okay," Marie replied, stepping aside. "Come in."

They sat at the small kitchen table, sunlight spilling in through the window. For a moment, neither of them spoke.

"I was worried about you," Catherine finally said. "We all were. Your phone was going straight to voicemail."

"I know," Marie said calmly. "I saw the calls."

"You okay?" Catherine asked.

Marie nodded. "I wasn't, but I am now."

Catherine hesitated. "Last night, that wasn't supposed to happen like that."

"I know," Marie said. "But it did."

Catherine sighed. "I don't know what got into Brielle. That wasn't right. It wasn't her place."

Marie looked at Catherine, steady and composed. "And that's why I'm not interested in talking to her right now."

Catherine blinked. "You don't want to hear her out?"

"No," Marie said simply. "Not today. Not tomorrow. Maybe not ever. I didn't deserve that," Marie continued. "And I'm not going to sit around while someone tries to figure out why they felt entitled to disrespect me."

Catherine nodded slowly. "I understand that."

"I'm not mad," Marie added. "I'm just clear." She stood up, grabbing her bag.

"Last night showed me something," she said. "And when people show you who they are, or how they feel about you, you don't argue with it."

Catherine reached over and squeezed Marie's hand.

"I'm proud of you," she said. "For walking away."

Marie smiled faintly. "Me too."

Marie headed toward the door, paused, and turned back. "I'm choosing peace," she said. "And I'm not negotiating that. I am done!"

123

Catherine smiled. "I got you."

Chapter Thirty-Two

Marie stepped off the plane, the warm southern air greeting her as she made her way through the airport doors. And there he was, Terrence, standing tall with a smile that could light up a room.

"Hello, Beautiful," he said, his voice smooth and warm. "You look amazing, just like I knew you would."

Marie felt her cheeks flush. "Thank you so much, Terrence. I'm so excited to be here!"

"And I'm excited for you to be here," he said, his eyes locked onto hers. "So, do you want to go to your room first, or should we grab some lunch? I have a few things planned for today, but we can always do them tomorrow. Everything depends on you."

Marie beamed. "I want to do everything! I'm not tired at all. I came ready to have a great time, so whatever you have planned, I'm all in."

"Perfect," Terrence said. "First, I want to take you to Eddie and Ruby's for some fish. I know you've had great fish before, because y'all have Get and Go in Omaha, Nebraska. I actually tried it with my daughter, and it was really good. But now, I want you to try ours."

Marie grinned. "I'm up for that!"

As they drove, their conversation flowed effortlessly. They laughed and shared stories, and before she knew it, they had arrived at Eddie and Ruby's. The smell of perfectly seasoned fish filled the air as they placed their orders; catfish and fries for Marie, a carp sandwich with fries for Terrence. They found a quiet spot nearby, parked, and dug in.

"This fish is amazing," Marie said between bites. "The seasoning is perfect, and the fries? Just the right amount of salt, not too much, not too little. I love it!"

Terrence chuckled. "I'm glad you're enjoying it. I always get the carp because I love how meaty it is, but the catfish is just as good. I wanted you to experience the lunch I get at least twice a week."

"Well, I see why you come here often," Marie said, savoring another bite.

After finishing their meal, Terrence drove toward Jackson State University. Marie spotted a large sign and turned to him with wide eyes.

"Wait, this is your college?" Marie asked.

"Yep," Terrence said proudly.

"You went to college too? Wow!"

"I have a bachelor's degree in business management. I went to college straight out of high school, before the military.

"It's so nice! The whole city has this country-like feel, it's so different from Omaha."

Terrence nodded. "Yeah, it's a different vibe, but it grows on you."

As they pulled up to park, Marie noticed a crowd forming on the campus.

"Whoa, there are so many people here!" she said.

"Yeah, there's an event happening today on the yard," Terrence said. "They're about to do a step show. I think you're gonna love it."

"A step show? We used to have those in high school!" Marie said excitedly.

Terrence smirked. "Oh, trust me, this is nothing like what you saw in high school. Come on, let's check it out."

Terrence took Marie's hand, leading her toward the yard, where music blasted through speakers. The energy was electric. Sororities and fraternities filled the space, stepping in perfect sync, and their movements sharp and commanding. Marie was in awe.

"I love watching them perform!" Marie said. "One of my friends almost joined a sorority, but she didn't. My best friend, though, he's a Kappa Alpha Psi! Did I say that right?"

Terrence chuckled. "Yeah, you got it. The Kappas are the ones with red and white canes. And the guys in purple? Those are the Ques. They bring the hype."

Marie's eyes lit up as she spotted them in action. "Oh my gosh, I love watching them jump and move all over the place!"

"Yeah, the Ques are wild," Terrence said, laughing. "But let me introduce you to my brothers." He led Marie over to a group of men in royal blue and pure white. "These are my Phi Beta Sigma brothers," he said, shaking hands with them in a way only they understood.

Marie watched in amazement as the Phi Beta Sigma's suddenly broke into a step routine. And then, just when she thought she'd seen it all, Terrence jumped right in.

She gasped. "Oh my God, Terrence, you never told me you were in a fraternity!"

He grinned mid-step. "It didn't come up," he said with a wink.

Marie laughed, completely caught up in the energy of it all. The music, the unity, and the excitement. It was unlike anything she had ever experienced.

"This is incredible!" Marie said. "I feel like I just walked into the best party of the year!"

"And we're just getting started," Terrence said.

After the step show, Terrence led Marie to the campus bookstore. "Have you ever thought about joining a sorority?" he asked.

Marie shook her head. "No, that never crossed my mind."

"You should think about it," he said. "Having a community to support you is a major win."

Marie hesitated. "I guess I could look into it."

Terrence smiled. "You should. And since your best friend is a Kappa, that means he's a brother to Sigma Gamma Rho. Honestly, you seem like a Sigma Gamma Rho woman."

Marie raised an eyebrow. "Oh really? And why is that?"

Terrence looked into her eyes. "Because you're classy, confident, hardworking, fun, and so doggone beautiful."

Marie felt a warmth rush through her as she reached out and hugged Terrence. "Wow, I wasn't expecting all that, but I appreciate it."

"It's just the truth," Terrence said simply.

※※※※※※※※※※※※※※※※

That night, Marie and Terrence got dressed in all white for the Greek party. As soon as they stepped in, the energy was alive. The room was filled with elegant, well-dressed people, the music was perfect, and the food, bite-sized hors d'oeuvres, was delicious. They sipped sodas and punch, danced, laughed, and soaked in the night. Marie had never had so much fun.

When they finally left at 2:00 AM, Terrence walked Marie to her hotel room. "I'll see you at 11:00 AM for brunch," he said, gently tucking a strand of hair behind her ear. "Make sure you get some good sleep, you traveled, walked the yard, and partied. I know you're tired, Beautiful."

Marie smiled. "Thank you so much for today, Terrence. It was amazing. I truly had the best time ever, and I can't wait to see what tomorrow brings."

"Me neither," Terrence said, kissing Marie's forehead. "Goodnight, Beautiful."

As Terrence walked away, Marie closed her door, her heart was full.

This vacation was going to be unforgettable.

Chapter Thirty-Three

Let me tell y'all something, tonight was different. I mean, I don't even know if I have the right words, but I know I've never felt like this before. Not from any man I've ever dealt with.

See, I've been so used to the drama and the foolishness, the hood games, the lies, the little slick disrespect they think we don't notice. I've gotten so used to having my guard up that it became my normal. Always watching my back. Always ready in case some woman came at me sideways. Always expecting chaos to come with love, like they're some package deal.

But tonight? Tonight was peace. Tonight was soft, it was safe, it was exactly what I didn't even know I needed.

Terrence whew! He moves differently. He's not loud about it, and he's not performing. He's just a man. He opened my door, looked me in the eye, and made me feel seen without making me feel exposed. And when he brought me back to my room? He didn't push for anything. He didn't act as if I owed him because we had a good time. He hugged me, kissed my forehead, told me goodnight, and said he'd see me tomorrow.

Y'all, who does that?

I'm telling you, I've never met a man like this. And you better believe I see God's hand all over this. Lord, I see You. Thank You for showing me I don't have to settle for the same old nonsense. Thank You for raising my awareness, for reminding me that my worth is higher than the way I've been letting myself be treated. And thank You for sending someone, whether he's here for a reason, a season, or forever, to show me how it feels to be treated right.

This man has me rethinking everything. Raising my standards even higher. Protecting this peace with my whole heart. And the crazy thing is, I don't even know what he has planned for tomorrow. But I've got a feeling it's going to be so good. Better than good.

Chapter Thirty-Four

Marie couldn't wipe the smile from her face. Every step she took, every move she made, that smile stayed with her. She got in the shower, letting the warm water wash over her, still replaying the night in her mind. She slipped into her pajamas, climbed into bed, and all the while she was daydreaming about Terrence, still in disbelief that she had met a man like that.

Because truth be told, Marie had never met a man before, not like this. It had always been the same old story, hood dudes, game players, and smooth talkers with nothing solid to offer. But Terrence, he was different. And Marie was just happy; genuinely happy, that things were going so well. She reached over to her phone and dialed Catherine.

Ring, ring.

"Hey, girl, what's up, Marie?" Catherine answered.

Marie couldn't hold back her excitement. "Catherine, you know how I told you Terrence was a man? Well, girl, he is such a gentleman. I mean, we went on this date, and it was perfect. The whole time I was laughing, smiling, and at peace. I felt happy, I felt comfortable, and I felt safe. And you know I've never hung out with a man where I didn't feel like I had to watch my back, checking behind me to see who's coming, and looking around to see who might be ready to start drama just because of who I'm with. There was none of that. It was peaceful."

Marie paused for a moment, taking a deep breath as if she could still feel that peace in her bones. "It's like he's the kind of man who doesn't bring drama, like his whole goal is to make sure you're happy. Girl, I could just hug him right now. And on top of that, when he brought me back to my room, he didn't push for anything. He hugged me, kissed me on my forehead, and told me 'Goodnight, I'll see you tomorrow.' Who does that?"

Catherine's voice lit up. "Marie, that's amazing! I don't even know what kind of man that is. That's those down-south gentlemen we've always heard about. I mean, he is from Jackson, Mississippi. That's crazy. I love this for you! I've never experienced that myself."

Marie laughed softly. "I can't believe it, Catherine. I could talk about this all night."

"No, you couldn't," Catherine teased, and they both burst out laughing.

Marie sighed happily. "Tomorrow? I don't even know what he's got planned, but I can't wait. No matter what it is, I'm going to take it all in with a smile, love it, and appreciate it, because I don't know this life. But I love it. And I appreciate it. I think it's amazing."

Catherine's tone softened. "Girl, I am so happy for you."

"I just had to call you," Marie said. "I know I always share my ups and downs and all the messy stuff, but I wanted to share this. This amazing moment. Because I'm still in disbelief. I'm going to bed feeling like I'm on cloud nine, and I've never been on cloud nine before. Now? I don't ever want to leave. This right here is going to change my whole outlook on life. I thought I'd already raised my standards, but baby, my expectations just went up."

"Well, OK, girl," Catherine said, smiling through the phone. "Make sure you call me tomorrow after everything. I need to know what y'all do, because how is he going to top this off?"

Marie laughed. "That's exactly what I'm wondering! He could send me home right now and I'd still be grinning from ear to ear. I'm just excited."

"Alright, girl. I love you," Catherine said.

"Love you too, Cat. Talk to you tomorrow. Bye."

Marie hung up the phone, curled up under the covers, and closed her eyes, still smiling.

Chapter Thirty-Five

Ring. Ring. Ring.

The phone kept ringing on the nightstand. By the fifth ring, Marie finally grabbed it.

"Hello?" she said groggily.

"What's up, Sweet Thing?" Dupree's voice boomed through the speaker, music and loud voices spilling in the background. "How you doing? You sound asleep. The night is young!"

"What's up, Dupree?" Marie replied, rubbing her eyes. "No, the night is old and I'm tired. I was asleep."

"Don't sound so disappointed," Dupree teased. "Normally you be all excited to hear from me. What's up? Where you at? Who you with? You must got a man. Better not have a man." He laughed, but his tone was probing.

"I'm just laying down, Dupree. I had a long day. I was asleep."

"Where you at?"

"I'm out of town. I came on vacation to hang out."

"To hang out?"

"Yeah."

"Where you on vacation at?"

"I'm in Jackson, Mississippi," Marie said, still half-asleep.

"Jackson, Mississippi?" Dupree repeated it slowly. "Wait, you sleeping? You ain't never told me that before. Usually, you get up and talk to me. Wait a minute!" his voice sharpened, "You laying next to somebody?"

"No, Dupree! I'm not laying next to anybody. Why would I be? I told you, I'm on vacation."

"You sound distant. And disappointed. But it's all good," Dupree said, now clearly annoyed.

"I'm just tired. I've got a whole day planned tomorrow, and it starts early. I need to get some rest, Dupree. Calm down."

"Okay, Marie. I'll talk to you. I'll call you tomorrow. I'm out."

"Goodnight," Marie said flatly, hanging up.

Chapter Thirty-Six

Dupree sat there with the phone still in his hand, staring at the dark screen like it had just betrayed him.

"What the hell was that?" he muttered under his breath. "Marie distant? With me? Nah! I ain't never heard her sound like that before; not with me, not Marie." Dupree leaned back in his seat, with the laughter and loud music from the club still spilling in from outside, but now it felt far away.

"She didn't even sound happy to hear my voice," he said, shaking his head. "Did I piss her off? Did I say something wrong? I don't know, man, I don't know." These thoughts hit Dupree hard.

"Wait. Is she out there with some dude? In Jackson, Mississippi? She didn't even explain why she's there. She just yelled, I'm on vacation." He rubbed his jaw, the confusion knotting tighter in his chest. "Marie don't act like that with me. Ever. I'm her person. And now what? I can't even call her?"

Dupree let out a heavy sigh, the disappointment hanging on his shoulders. "Nah, this don't feel right. I ain't never been in this position before. Never. I don't even know how to move right now."

His voice dropped, almost like he was talking to himself in the mirror.

"Alright, Dupree, get yourself together. You been drinking. You been smoking. Your head ain't right. You feelin' delusional, and when you feel like this, nothing makes sense."

He glanced around the parking lot, his eyes unfocused. "As a matter of fact, I don't even like this feeling. I've never felt like this before. Not about anybody. Not even about Marie."

Dupree gripped the steering wheel tighter, the frustration giving way to exhaustion. "Alright! I'm out. I'm done for the night."

Dupree rolled up his windows, turned down his music until the car was wrapped in silence, and just sat there for a moment, staring through the windshield like the answers might show up in the streetlights. Then he pulled off slow, with his mind still replaying her voice; flat, tired, and distant.

By the time Dupree got home, the weight in his chest hadn't lifted. He walked inside, dropped his keys on the counter without looking, and collapsed onto the couch. No TV. No music. Just him, the quiet, and that lingering question in his head.

What just happened with Marie?

Eventually, his eyes closed, not because his mind was at peace, but because his body couldn't keep fighting the confusion anymore.

Chapter Thirty-Seven

Ring, ring.

"Hey, Terrence."

"Hey, Marie," his voice came through, warm and steady. "I was just calling to let you know to come outside. I'm here."

"You're here?" Marie said, already smiling.

"Yep."

"Okay, I'm on my way."

They hung up, and Marie's heart was already racing. She'd been ready for hours, makeup perfect, hair laid just right, but now, the anticipation was real. She slipped on her shoes and practically floated to the door.

When she stepped outside, there he was, Terrence, straddling a sleek black motorcycle, with the chrome gleaming under the Mississippi sun.

"Oh my goodness, a motorcycle?" Marie said laughing, with her surprise impossible to hide.

Terrence chuckled. "Yep. You're ridin' with me today."

"Wait, what am I supposed to do? Just hop on?"

"Of course," he grinned. "And I figured you might have on some pretty shoes, so I brought you these shoe covers. That way, your feet won't get hurt while we ride."

Marie couldn't help but laugh and shake her head. "You thought of everything."

She was still smiling as she climbed on the motorcycle behind Dupree. She'd never done anything like this before, but there was no fear, just curiosity and excitement. I'm going to take it all in, she thought. I'm going to enjoy this.

Terrence drove with care, steady and smooth, nothing like the reckless riders she'd seen before. Ten minutes later, they pulled up in front of the Mississippi Civil Rights Museum.

Marie's eyes widened. "Is this where we're going?"

"Yeah," Terrence said. "I want to show you some history, show you what we're about in Mississippi. What we've fought for. What we're still fighting for."

Marie's heart warmed. "I love museums. I love history. This, this is special. Thank you."

Inside, they wandered through the powerful, interactive exhibits. Marie was struck by the depth of the storytelling, the Freedom Rides, the speeches, and the photographs that explained decades of struggle and resilience.

"My Aunt Bertha Calloway owns the Black Museum in Omaha," Marie explained. "I remember hearing about the Freedom Rides growing up. Seeing this here, it's powerful."

Terrence smiled. "I didn't even know Nebraska had a Black Museum. That's amazing. And you know your history. That's rare."

For hours, they explored, laughed, and reflected. There was no rush, just two people fully present with each other.

When they stepped back outside, Terrence turned to Marie. "Alright, beautiful. Let's eat. I know you like burgers, so I'm taking you to one of our staples, Stamps Super Burgers. It's the best burger you'll ever have."

Marie grinned. "I'm in. I love burgers."

Again, Terrence rode with care, and soon they were at Stamps. Marie's eyes went wide when her super cheeseburger with bacon and fries arrived. They ate, they laughed, and conversation flowed like they'd known each other for years.

As the evening wound down, Terrence looked at Marie seriously. "I know you leave in the morning. I just want to say thank you, for coming, for trusting me enough to spend your time here. I've enjoyed you. I hope this isn't the last time I see you."

Marie smiled, her heart full. "It definitely won't be. You've opened my eyes to so much. From the moment I got off the plane, you've been nothing but kind, genuine, and intentional. This is something I've never experienced, and it feels good. Really good."

Terrence nodded. "Well, I'll take you to the airport in the morning. And we'll figure out the next time, whether I'm coming to you or you're coming back here. I'd like you to meet my daughter one day. I want this friendship to grow."

"Me too," Marie said softly.

They hugged, and Terrence left, leaving Marie with a smile that wouldn't fade.

Back in her room, Marie kicked off her shoes, stretched out on the bed, and closed her eyes. The day had been rich with history, laughter, and genuine connection. Her spirit felt light. Her heart felt safe. And before she knew it, she drifted into a peaceful nap, resting not just from the day, but in the joy of knowing she had just experienced something rare and real.

Chapter Thirty-Eight

Terrence arrived at Marie's hotel right at 8:15 a.m., just like he said he would. He stood at her door, already reaching for her bags when she opened it.

"Good morning," he said with a warm smile.

"Good morning," Marie replied, with a soft but happy voice. "You're right on time."

"I told you I would be," Terrence said, lifting her bags easily. "Just like when you got here."

Marie laughed. "So consistent. I like that."

They walked to the car, and once they were on the road, the silence didn't feel awkward, it felt comfortable.

"This weekend went by way too fast," Marie said, looking out the window.

"It really did," Terrence replied. "But it was a good one. A really good one."

"Thank you," Marie said sincerely. "For everything. For being thoughtful. For being you."

"No, thank you," Terrence said. "For trusting me. For coming. I'm glad you did."

They smiled at each other, replaying moments in their heads: the museum, the laughs, the food, and the peace.

"So," Terrence said, glancing over at her, "what are we thinking for next time?"

"Well," Marie said thoughtfully, "I think it's only right that you come to Omaha."

Terrence nodded. "I'm good with that. About a month?"

"Yeah," Marie said, smiling. "That sounds perfect. I want you to meet my friends and my family."

Terrence raised his eyebrows slightly. "Your family?"

"Yes," Marie said confidently. "You're the kind of person I don't mind introducing to them."

"That means a lot," Terrence said quietly.

He paused for a moment, then said, "There's something else I want to do."

"What's that?" Marie asked.

Terrence picked up his phone. "I want you to meet my daughter."

Marie smiled. "I'd love that."

He dialed the number.

"Hey, sweetheart," Terrence said when she answered. "I'm with Marie."

"Hi," Imery said.

"Hi, Imery," Marie replied warmly.

"I just wanted y'all to meet," Terrence said. "I want you two to exchange numbers."

"That's fine," Imery said. "Nice to meet you, Marie."

"Nice to meet you too," Marie said. "I look forward to meeting you in person."

Numbers were exchanged, and Terrence smiled to himself.

"You don't have to wait until I visit for y'all to connect," he told his daughter. "She's going to be around for a while. She's a good person."

They hung up just as the airport came into view.

"Terrence," Marie said, her voice full, "you are truly amazing. I appreciate you so much."

"And you're amazing too," Terrence said. "More than you realized. I'm glad I met you. This weekend reminded me there are still good people in the world."

"Likewise," Marie said softly.

Terrence pulled up to the curb, got out, and placed Marie's bags on the sidewalk. They stood there for a moment, not rushing the goodbye.

He hugged her, then kissed her gently on the cheek.

"Until next time," he said.

"Until next time," Marie replied, smiling as she waved.

Terrence waved back, got in the car, and drove away.

Marie turned and walked into the airport, still smiling, carrying her bags, her peace, and the quiet joy of knowing this trip was ending in promise.

Chapter Thirty-Nine

I just want to say this to myself for a minute. I'm really proud of you.

This weekend showed me something I didn't even realize I was missing. I wasn't tense. I wasn't overthinking. I wasn't trying to read between the lines or protect my feelings every second. I was just present. And that's rare for me.

I'm so used to chaos feeling normal. I'm used to confusion, mixed signals, noise, and foolishness. I've spent so much time convincing myself that love, attention, or connection had to come with stress. But this time, it didn't. And that's what shook me.

I didn't feel rushed. I didn't feel pressured. I didn't feel like I had to perform or prove anything. I felt respected. I felt safe. And now I understand something deeper.

I'm not a person who just talks about God, ever, but now I get it. I understand why my parents always said, "You'll know when it's God." Because nothing about this felt forced. It just flowed. That peace? That wasn't accidental.

I don't know what's next, and that's okay. I'm just grateful that God showed me there's more than what I've been settling for; more than the patterns, more than the drama, and more than the familiar disappointments.

This experience raised the bar for me, and I'm not apologizing for that. I'm thankful, I'm hopeful, and I'm excited. And for the first time in a long time, I am truly happy.

Chapter Forty

Ring Ring Ring!

"What's up Marie," Charlotte asked.

"A whole lot of everything is up, Charlotte. Oh my goodness."

"Please tell me, Marie. This has got to be great!"

"When I tell you I had the most amazing time of my life," Marie said, her voice still full with excitement, "I really mean that. I had the most amazing time of my life. Terrence showed out. He treated me like a queen, no shortcuts, no slacking, no half-stepping. He was so good to me. I mean, I expected him to be nice, but this? This was unbelievable."

Charlotte laughed. "Okay, see, that's what I'm talking about. You're talking in feelings, not details. I need details."

"I'm trying to get it out," Marie said, laughing too. "I'm just still on a high. But okay, details. First, he took me to this fish house they have down there. When I tell you that fish was amazing, Girl. Amazing. They showed out with that food. I'm still thinking about it."

"Mmm," Charlotte said. "Okay, keep going."

"Then we went to a museum. And, don't laugh, we went on a motorcycle ride."

"A motorcycle?" Charlotte gasped. "You don't even like motorcycles!"

"I know! And that's the crazy part," Marie said. "But when I tell you I felt free, I felt free. No fear. No anxiety. Just wind, peace, and joy. Life felt so good at that moment. I can't even fully explain it. I'm still in awe, and that's why I had to call you, because I'm still up here, and I know once I unwind, reality is going to come knocking."

"And you don't want to come down," Charlotte said softly.

"No never! I really don't," Marie admitted. "But what I'm learning from Terrence, whether he's my person or not, is that there's so much more to life than what I've been settling for. I've been settling for foolishness, and I didn't even have to."

Charlotte was quiet for a second. "That's powerful."

"And remember what my dad used to say?" Marie continued. "That the man meant for me would be even better to me than he was. And I didn't think that was possible, because my dad set the bar high. But this weekend? I got a glimpse. Just a glimpse."

Charlotte smiled through the phone. "Wow."

"Oh, and listen," Marie added quickly. "I'm home now. The flight was smooth."

"Wait, hold on," Charlotte jumped in. "So, what happened? Did he spend the night?"

"No, ma'am," Marie said firmly. "He didn't. He didn't even try. That wasn't part of his plan at all. He just wanted me to be at peace, to be happy, and to enjoy myself. And that's exactly what I did."

Charlotte exhaled. "That's different."

"And one more thing," Marie said, her voice lighting up again. "I've never been to a Black college before. He took me to one. I watched the sororities and fraternities show out, Charlotte. When I tell you I've never seen anything like that in my life, I mean that. He's part of a fraternity, and when they got together? Baby. I was amazed."

Charlotte laughed. "You sound like a whole different person."

"I feel like one too," Marie said honestly. "I feel like I'm in a new place. And I don't want to go backwards. I don't even want to think about going backwards."

"Don't," Charlotte said gently. "Take it like going to church. You get the word, you feel lifted, and you don't let the world steal it when you walk back out."

"I know," Marie said. "And you're right. I really do feel like God showed me something. Like He let me see what's possible. And now? I'm just tired, in a good way. I just want to lay down, rest, and sit with it."

Charlotte smiled. "Marie, you inspired me. I didn't even know men like that really existed. I'm so happy for you."

"Thank you," Marie said softly. "I love you."

"I love you too," Charlotte replied.

They said their goodbyes, and the call ended, leaving Marie full, grateful, and forever changed by the glimpse she had been given.

Chapter Forty-One

The celebration was set for Carter's Café on 24th and Lake, a place rich with history, flavor, and heart. Catherine had quietly rented out the space, keeping everything intimate and intentional; no crowds. Just love. About twenty-five of their closest friends and family were invited; people who mattered, people who knew their story.

Marie and Tasha arrived early, which for them meant right on time, doing what they always did: handling business with love and intention. Hunter green and gold set the tone from the start, colors chosen with care; green for growth and stability, gold for celebration and promise.

Balloons rose in soft clusters, with shimmering gold catching the light, and deep green grounding the space. Tables were aligned just right, each one crowned with beautifully displayed Happy Birthday centerpieces, elegant, thoughtful, and perfectly placed; quietly pulling the room together like the final note in a well-written song.

As they worked, the café began to change. What had once been an ordinary space slowly warmed into something special, something welcoming. There was a quiet excitement in the air; nothing loud, just that feeling you get when you know something special is coming. And in the back room, the second surprise waited; hidden, patient, and certain of its moment.

The party officially started at 2:30, but by 2:15, like clockwork, guests began trickling in. Laughter filled the room. Hugs were exchanged. Conversations overlapped. Everyone knew something special was coming, they just didn't know how special.

Carter's Café catered the food, and they did not disappoint. The spread was pure comfort and culture: their famous fried and smothered chicken legs, creamy garlic mashed potatoes, candied yams that tasted like love, green beans with potatoes done just right, and banana pudding that didn't stand a chance. Grape and lemonade Kool-Aid flowed freely, because some traditions don't need upgrading.

Ms. Lucy Carter herself baked the cake, a beautiful half-and-half masterpiece. One side read Happy Birthday, the other Congratulations, Dad.

At 2:45, Catherine walked in with Dakar, just as planned. She told him they were simply going to lunch. As soon as they stepped through the door, the room erupted.

"SURPRISE!"

Dakar froze, then smiled, then laughed, then hugged Catherine, like he'd just won the lottery. He couldn't believe it. A surprise party? For him? He was overwhelmed with gratitude, soaking it all in, greeting guests, shaking hands, and hugging friends.

Marie stood up and made the announcement that Dakar and Catherine would eat first, then the guests. Plates were filled, tables were lively, and the room buzzed with joy. After everyone ate, Marie led a few lighthearted games, keeping the energy high and the laughter flowing.

Then came the birthday song. Everyone sang as Dakar beamed. He was genuinely thankful; grateful for life, for love, and for the people in that room.

That's when Catherine asked for the microphone. Marie passed it to her and stepped back. Catherine took a breath and looked straight at Dakar.

"First, I just want you to know how loved you are," she said. "Not just today, but always. You're respected. You show up, as a man, as a friend, as a son, as a brother. People can count on you."

Catherine smiled slightly and shook her head. "And yes, you're successful. Not just in what you do, but in who you are. Your character speaks before you ever say a word." She paused, letting that sit.

"And, we wanted to add one more thing to your life."

The room went quiet.

"Marie, would you please roll it out?" Marie brought out the gift bag from the back room. At the same moment, Catherine opened her jacket to reveal a shirt that read: Happy Birthday, We're Having a Baby, while she held up the gifts: a baby hat, tiny onesie, little gloves, and baby socks.

The room exploded. Cheers. Gasps. Tears. Applause.

Dakar yelled, "Oh my God! We're having a baby! I'm having a baby, with my best friend, my high school sweetheart, the love of my life!" Dakar took a step forward and dropped to one knee.

"Catherine," he said softly, "it's always been you."

The room went still.

"You make me better. You hold me accountable. You believe in me, even when I doubt myself. You love me honestly." Dakar swallowed and smiled. "Doing life with you feels right. Becoming parents together feels sacred."

He took Catherine's hand. "Will you be my wife?"

Catherine was already crying, but when she said yes, the room erupted all over again. Tears, cheers, and full hearts. The cake was cut, laughter lingered, and it was one of those days people talk about years later.

A day layered with love, a surprise birthday party, a surprise baby announcement, and a surprise proposal; all in one.

Marie's phone rang. She glanced at it. Imery? Terrence's daughter, this must be important.

"Hello?"

"Hey, Marie! It's Imery. How are you?"

"I'm doing great! How about you, Sweetheart?"

"I'm good. I was calling for my dad. He sent a surprise gift for you and wanted me to bring it by."

"Oh my goodness, that's so sweet! I'm not busy. When were you thinking?"

"Well, I was hoping I could drop it off in the morning?"

"Of course! That works perfectly. I'll be home."

"My dad gave me your address so I have it, so I'll just come by then."

"Perfect. See you in the morning, Imery."

"Thanks, Marie! Bye!"

Marie hung up and smiled, then turned back to the celebration.

§§§§§§§§§§§§§§§§§§

As the celebration wound down, most of the guests stayed behind to help with the cleanup. Laughter lingered in the air, music was low, chairs were being stacked, and plates were gathered; it was just one of those quiet endings that always felt comforting.

Marie was wiping down a table when one of those sharp chest pains suddenly hit her. She leaned forward suddenly, pressing her hand to her chest. "Oh no, not again," she whispered.

Catherine looked up immediately. "What's wrong, Marie? You, okay?"

"I'm fine," Marie said quickly, though her voice wavered. "I just felt another sharp pain in my chest."

"Another?" Catherine asked, with concern settling in her eyes.

"Yeah," Marie admitted. "They've been happening for a little while now. Not all the time, just at random moments."

Tasha had walked up just in time to hear that. "Wait. You're having chest pains, and you haven't said anything?" she said, arms crossing. "That's not smart, Marie."

"I'm okay, y'all," Marie insisted. "I really am."

From across the room, Brielle glanced over, noticing the tension, but this time, she stayed silent.

"I already made an appointment," Marie added. "I'm going to the doctor tomorrow afternoon. I'll be fine."

Catherine exhaled and rolled her eyes. "Okay, Marie. You better go."

"You know what happened to my aunt," Tasha said gently, but firmly.

"Don't do that, Tasha," Marie replied, trying to lighten the moment.

They all let out a small, uneasy chuckle.

"I'm serious, though," Tasha said. "Promise me you're going."

"I know," Marie nodded. "I am."

With that, the conversation faded. They finished cleaning, but quietly and thoughtfully, each of them were stealing glances at Marie, with concern tucked behind their practiced smiles. The room was clean. But the feeling lingered.

This was a beautiful day and a complete success. This was a good reminder that love, when it's real, shows up big.

Chapter Forty-Two

I'm really happy. I'm so thankful that everything went so well today. It honestly couldn't have gone any better. We set this up perfectly. Everybody worked together, showed up, and made it happen for Catherine. And the proposal, watching that moment unfold, knowing it was a surprise for everyone, and then realizing Dakar was planning to surprise her with a ring, just wow. That was beautiful. It was everything. Truly unforgettable. The day itself was amazing.

Now, if I'm being honest, and I am! I didn't love the moment Brielle walked into the room. And I know that's okay, because I didn't start whatever that was, and I don't owe her anything. She owes me an apology, but even with that, I don't want it. I'm good.

I don't need explanations. I don't need closure. I don't need to revisit it. Brielle can keep her distance, and I'm perfectly fine keeping mine. I don't ever have to be in the same space with her again, and if I am, I'll stay classy. I'll mind my words. I'll protect my peace. That part is non-negotiable.

I still don't know what shifted or why it shifted. I don't know where it came from. But I know something changed. And one day, it'll make sense, it always does.

Today just isn't that day, and that's okay too. Right now, I'm choosing gratitude. This was a good day. A really good day.

And now? I'm ready to go home, lie down, and rest in that. Except, I've got to stop pretending this chest pain is nothing. It's not the first time, and it doesn't feel smaller; it feels sharper. I keep telling myself it's just stress, because a lot keeps happening. But then I hear my parents' voices in my head, reminding me, over and over, to get myself checked. And the thought hits me hard: I would hate to ignore this and leave them with a what-if.

Okay. Now I've officially scared myself. No more brushing it off. No more waiting. I'm going to the ER.

Chapter Forty-Three

On the drive to the hospital, Marie called Charlotte and Catherine and told them to meet her at the ER at Bergan Mercy.

By the time she arrived, muscle memory took over. She checked in. They weighed her. Took her blood pressure. Everybody knew her, because this was her hospital, her workplace. Except this time, she wasn't working. She was the patient.

Marie sat on the bed, with her feet dangling, and her heart still feeling tight in her chest. She tried to stay calm, but the quiet made everything louder: her breathing, her thoughts, and the what-ifs she had been pushing away for weeks.

A few minutes later, Charlotte rushed in. "Marie, what is going on?" she asked, eyes wide. "You do not go to the hospital, ever. So, what just happened?"

Marie exhaled. "I don't know. I've been having these chest pains. Today, they were worse. And I scared myself into coming."

"How long has this been going on?"

"For a minute."

"A minute?" Charlotte's voice went up. "You work here. Why would you..."

"Charlotte," Marie cut her off gently. "I know. I just didn't want to deal with it."

Before Charlotte could respond, Catherine walked in. "Hey, y'all, why are we in the ER?"

Marie leaned back against the pillow. "Remember earlier, when we were cleaning up, and I leaned over the table? That pain has been happening, and today was just the worst one."

Catherine frowned. "And you didn't say anything?"

"I know I know, but today after the party, I kept thinking, what if I ignore this and something happens? What if I could've saved myself and didn't? I didn't want tonight to be that night."

Charlotte nodded slowly. "I'm glad you came."

Not long after, Dr. Xayden walked in, one of Marie's colleagues.

"Marie," Dr. Xayden said, half concerned, half incredulous. "What are you doing here?"

"I've been having chest pains. For a while. Today was the worst."

He raised an eyebrow. "And you didn't come sooner?"

169

Marie shook her head. "I didn't want to. But I'm here now."

"Good," Dr. Xayden said firmly. "We're running everything so we can figure this out." And they did just that: CT scan, MRI, x-rays, ultrasound, and bloodwork.

Marie was wheeled in and out, surrounded by machines she normally helped other people navigate. This time, she said nothing. She just waited.

After nearly three hours, Dr. Xayden returned.

"Marie," he said, pulling up a stool, "we ran every test we could think of. Everything looks normal."

Marie blinked. "Everything?"

"Everything."

Charlotte and Catherine let out quiet breaths of relief.

"There is one more thing," Dr. Xayden added thoughtfully. "We should run a pregnancy test."

Marie laughed nervously. "I would be very disappointed if I were pregnant."

Catherine looked at her sideways. "I wouldn't. We could go through this together."

Charlotte smiled softly. "A baby wouldn't be a bad thing."

"For y'all," Marie said. "But for me? I'm not ready."

"I'll have the nurses come give you a urine test," Dr. Xayden said.

A nurse came in twenty minutes later, and Marie went to the restroom for her urine test.

They waited.

When Dr. Xayden came back, he was smiling. "Well," he said, "Marie, I think you're going to be surprised."

Marie's heart skipped. "Please tell me it's negative."

Dr. Xayden chuckled. "You might want to sit down."

"I'm already sitting."

"Congratulations, Marie," he said gently. "You're pregnant."

The room went silent.

Charlotte's hand flew to her mouth. Catherine stared. Marie just sat there.

"Oh," Marie finally said. "Okay."

Shock washed over her, no panic, no tears, just disbelief.

"I don't know what I'm going to do," Marie said quietly. "But I'll figure it out."

Chapter Forty-Four

The drive home was quiet. No music. No phone calls. No distractions. Marie pulled out of the hospital parking lot and let the night carry her forward. The streetlights blurred as she drove, each one passing like a thought she wasn't ready to hold onto yet.

Pregnant! The word sat there: present, heavy, and unreal. Marie didn't cry. She didn't smile. She didn't panic. She just existed with it.

Her mind kept replaying everything instead, like that would help it make sense. The chest pain! The stress! The way life had been speeding up lately! Her parents getting back together! Marcellus! Terrence! Dupree! The argument at the restaurant! The celebration! The ER! It felt like too much had happened too fast, like life had stacked moment after moment without asking if she was ready.

"I don't even know how we got here," Marie whispered to herself, with her eyes fixed on the road.

She tried to calculate the time, remember dates, and line things up logically, but nothing wanted to land neatly. Every thought led to another, and none of them finished their sentence. Her chest didn't hurt anymore. That alone made her uneasy.

"So that's what it was," she murmured. "Or maybe that wasn't it at all."

Marie thought about how close she'd come to brushing the pain off again, about how easily she could've gone home and laid down like she planned, and about how many times she'd told herself she was fine.

"I really could've ignored this," she said quietly. "I almost did."

The car felt smaller now. The silence heavier. Marie thought about responsibility, not in a scary way, just in a real way. The kind of responsibility that shifts something inside of you before you even understand why.

"I'm not ready," she admitted. "But I guess being ready isn't the requirement." That thought stayed with her longer than the rest.

She pulled into her driveway and sat there for a moment, with her engine still running, and her hands resting on the steering wheel. Everything in her life felt the same, and completely different at the same time; no conclusions, no decisions, and no plans; just awareness.

"Okay," Marie said softly. "One thing at a time."

She turned off the car, stepped out into the quiet night, and walked inside, carrying a truth she wasn't ready to unpack yet, but no longer pretending it wasn't there. And for the first time in a long time, Marie didn't try to figure everything out. She just let herself be.

Chapter Forty-Five

Marie didn't turn on any lights when she walked into the house. She dropped her keys by the door, kicked off her shoes, and went straight to the bathroom. The shower water was hot, almost too hot, but she let it run over her anyway, like it might wash the night off her skin.

She stood there longer than usual. Not thinking. Not praying. Just letting the water fall. When she finally turned the water off, she wrapped herself in a towel, walked into her bedroom, and sat down on the edge of her bed. That's when it hit her again; not panic, not fear, just weight.

Marie sat there for a moment, then picked up the phone and called her parents.

"Hello?" her mom answered, "Marie?"

"Yeah, it's me."

"What's wrong, Baby?"

"I'm okay," Marie said softly. "I really am. I just need to tell y'all something."

Her dad, who was right next to her mother, listened on the line too. "Hey, Princess. We are here." Those words settled in Marie's chest more than anything else had all night.

"I went to the ER," Marie said. "These chest pains got worse today, and I finally went in."

Her mom exhaled slowly. "Thank you for going."

"They ran every test," Marie continued. "And everything came back normal."

"That's good," her dad said.

Marie paused, staring at the floor. "And then they ran a pregnancy test."

Silence.

"I'm pregnant."

Her mom didn't gasp and her dad didn't rush in with questions.

Then her mom spoke gently. "How are you feeling right now?"

"I don't even know yet," Marie said honestly. "I'm not breaking down. I'm just sitting here trying to let it all land."

Her dad's voice was steady. "You don't have to figure anything out tonight."

"I know," Marie said. "I just needed to hear y'all."

Her mom said softly, "This doesn't change who you are, and it doesn't mean you did anything wrong."

Marie swallowed. "I keep thinking about the chest pain. It's like my body was trying to get my attention."

"Sometimes it does," her dad said. "And sometimes God does too."

Marie leaned back on the bed, staring at the ceiling.

"We've told you before," her mom added, "when something doesn't feel right, listen. You listened this time."

"I almost didn't," Marie admitted.

"But you did," her dad said. "And we're proud of you."

Tears came quietly, not rushing, and not overwhelming, just enough to release what Marie had been holding in. "I don't know what I'm going to do yet," Marie said.

"You don't need to," her mom replied. "Tonight, you just need to rest."

"One step at a time," her dad said. "We'll walk with you."

Marie closed her eyes.

"Thank y'all," she whispered. "I just needed my parents."

"We know," her mom said. "That's why we're here."

When the call ended, Marie laid back on the bed, with her hands resting over her chest, and started to do something she never did, pray. God! I don't know what this means. I don't know what comes next. I'm not ready, but I'm here. Please steady me. Please cover what I can't control. Give me wisdom before answers, peace before understanding, and strength for whatever tomorrow asks of me.

Marie exhaled slowly, with her prayer trailing off before it finished, because there was nothing left to say, only the quiet of knowing that she wasn't alone. So, she stayed there, letting the silence speak the rest, and letting the moment sit with her, trusting that for right now, being still was enough.

Chapter Forty-Six

It was a little after six o'clock in the morning when Marie's doorbell pierced through her sleep. She sat straight up in bed, with her heart racing.

Oh my God, it's six in the morning. Who is ringing my doorbell? Her mind immediately went there. This better not be Vanessa. I swear, I am not in the mood for chaos today. I'm already carrying too much.

Marie slipped on her robe, slid her feet into her house shoes, and moved cautiously toward the door. Through the peephole, she saw a young girl standing on her porch, shoulders shaking, head bowed, crying so hard it sounded like her chest might cave in. Her stomach dropped. Who comes to someone's door crying like that?

"Who is it?" Marie called out, her voice tight.

"Is, is this Marie's house?" the girl asked through sobs.

"Yes. This is Marie," she answered, unlocking the door. "Hold on."

When the door opened, Marie was met by Imery. Her eyes were swollen and red, her face streaked with tears, her hands trembling as she clutched a sealed envelope.

"Oh my goodness," Marie whispered. "Imery, what's going on? Are you okay? Come in, Sweetheart." Marie guided Imery inside and helped her sit on the couch.

Imery tried to speak but could barely breathe through her sobbing. "I'm so sorry, Marie," she finally said.

"You're sorry?" Marie asked softly. "Why would you be sorry? What's happening?"

Imery held out the envelope with shaking hands.

"This, this is for you. From my dad."

Marie's chest tightened. "Okay, but are you okay? Do I need to call him? Or your mom? Talk to me, Imery."

Imery shook her head violently. "No! No, Marie." Imery took a deep, broken breath. Around three this morning, my dad was hit by a drunk driver."

Marie froze.

"He was riding his motorcycle home. He was only a few houses away. Almost there," Imery continued, her words coming apart. "Someone was speeding down the street. They didn't stop, and they didn't slow down. They hit my dad so hard he flew and hit the concrete." Her voice cracked completely. "They said he died on impact.

Marie gasped, a sound that came from somewhere deep and wounded. "Oh God, no. I'm so sorry. I don't even have words, Imery. Your dad, Terrence…"

"He sent this gift yesterday morning," Imery interrupted, pushing the envelope toward Marie again. "He told me, 'Make sure Marie gets this today or tomorrow.' I promised him I would."

Marie took the envelope, her hands trembling now too.

Marie pulled Imery into her arms, both of them were crying hard now.

"I don't have my dad anymore, Marie," Imery cried out. "He's gone. And I don't know how to say that out loud. I don't know how to live without my dad. Imery broke completely then.

Dr. Charmaine Marie is an educator, author, and advocate dedicated to empowering youth and families through knowledge, boundaries, and self-respect. As an Amazon Best-Selling Author, she writes with purpose across multiple genres, including children's self-love books, youth life-skills curricula and workbooks, and adult self-love and drama novels that explore healing, growth, and healthy relationships.

With a background in education and youth mentorship, Dr. Charmaine Marie is passionate about teaching life skills that are often overlooked but deeply necessary. Her work emphasizes personal boundaries, consent, healthy relationships, and the long-term impact of choices. She believes prevention begins with honest conversations, clear guidance, and adults who are willing to teach what matters before harm occurs.

Beyond writing, Dr. Charmaine Marie is a devoted mother, proud grandmother, community leader, and entrepreneur. She is the founder of Real LOVE Executive, a woman-owned luxury wine company, and continues to serve through education, advocacy, and leadership. Her mission is simple but powerful: to help raise informed, confident youth who grow into responsible, respectful, and successful adults.

We really appreciate you taking the time to read,

Love, Lessons, and the Game of Life Book 2:

The Becoming

Please do a review on Amazon.com

to let us know what you think.